L.O.B.S.T.E.R

L.O.B.S.T.E.R

Do you need him, to love him?

SHRADDHA NYATI

White Falcon
Publishing

www.whitefalconpublishing.com

L.O.B.S.T.E.R
Shraddha Nyati

www.whitefalconpublishing.com

Requests for permission should be addressed to
shraddha.nyati@gmail.com

ISBN - 978-1-63640-218-5

*To all those who have kept
loving in your heart.*

Your smile says it all.

"When two best friends fall in love with each other, it's like they experience the best of two worlds: friendship and love. But if only one of them falls, there is nothing left, neither friendship nor love. It rips them apart. After all, you cannot be in two places all at once."

ACKNOWLEDGMENT

Creating a story is no big deal but continuing to write it to see the end requires sheer patience, endless mugs of coffee, and nights filled with crazy dreams.

I cannot start without mentioning that guy in the car who was bobbing his head at a street light while I was walking towards a grocery store. He made me daydream, & that's when the first character came alive. But it would not have been possible to pen it down in black & white had it not been for COVID-19 lockdowns; which gave me ample hours to build upon my daydream.

My deepest, heartfelt gratitude to my younger sister, Urvi, who edited my draft with sheer perfection. It made me feel utterly paralysed grammatically speaking, seeing her mercilessly dissecting my sentences. She is my star & someone who can make me jealous by having fun with siblings other than me.

People who read my first draft & made me question my high opinion about romance. They autopsied my draft with all the human psychology they knew. Neti, and Aashay, I hope the characters in the final version are more flawed than the exceptional ones that I created in the first draft.

Shikha, who has always been the first one to discuss my blogs. You made me believe that not everybody can write & make the reader say, "Damn! I feel exactly the same!"

Jitesh, for believing that my thoughts are a source of wonder.

Zoya, for making fun of all the weird emotions I express through words & making me realize that not everybody will like what I write & that's okay.

My parents, both biological and non-biological, for always being there & letting me carelessly dream.

My brother, Manas, for all those letters he has sent me over these past few years.

My Nani, from whose life I derive great strength.

The entire team at White Falcon for being patient through the entire process & making my book come alive.

And ofcourse my husband, Shaurya, who has never read what I have written, because it is always more than one page & makes him overthink. I love you; it couldn't have been done without your busy schedule that left me with nothing but my thoughts & laptop. You have let me be the unadulterated version of myself, making it possible for me to express my emotions with purity.

You are my L.O.B.S.T.E.R ♡

And for the faith that makes me who I am!

Love
Shraddha ☺

Prologue

Bay St., Boothbay Harbor, Maine, U.S.A.
16th April 2019

"I can feel the distance between us." He says in his drowsy voice. "Whenever we spent time together, I never took any moment for granted. But now I feel I should have treasured those times even when we were not together; at least you were here, in the same city, closer to me."

"I am still there." She says with warmth in her tone.

"No. You aren't! You are in an entirely different country. You are at a place where I can't even reach. If not in the same city, had you been somewhere around, I would have come to you whenever I missed you. I know it's foolish, but at least I would like to know that I can come to you whenever I want."

"I will be visiting soon."

"Soon? Soon cannot be right now." The impatience in his voice was apparent.

"Switch on the video camera. Let's make *'soon'* right now."

"No. No." He tries to fight off his frustration.

"What? Why?" He doesn't speak for a while. She asks again, almost whispering, "Tell me why?"

"It's not about just looking at you. It's about feeling your presence. It's about holding your hands and feeling your heart that beats and makes mine beat too. It's about knowing that my world is right here, in my arms." His voice crackled into a sob.

She could hear his deep breathing, which was driving her insane.

"You don't understand what you do to me. You don't understand the presence of your smile in your eyes when you are right beside me, when I know I can kiss it broader or get lost in the map that your hands entail."

"I miss you too." She whispered.

"Then come, please." He insisted with all the love he can put in a few words in his husky voice, sending ripples across her soul.

"You are feeling this today because you are drunk. You will be fine tomorrow morning. Life would be back to its routine, and you will forget about all these intense feelings." She carefully tries to rationalize his feelings before she could let herself flow with them. She has been there so often, and she knew it never ended well for her.

"Are you kidding me? These feelings never go away. They have eternally housed in my heart and my life. And if you feel that it is just because I am drunk and will forget about these feelings in the morning, you are mistaken. You have no idea how much effort it takes to keep my mind away from your thoughts. They keep drifting to you. They want to be with you. Your thoughts consume me. They drive me insane. It's just like you used to say; it's difficult to live with them and without them."

"Are you ok?" She had started to worry now. He hardly expressed with such intensity.

"Of course not! I miss you like crazy. And the worst part is I cannot even come to see you." He said, exasperated.

"What's happening? You have never expressed so much."

"Because it scares you! Vulnerability scares you, just like right now. But that doesn't change what I feel for you. Every moment of my waking life is spent trying not to remember you. I wish we had more time. I wish I could have held on to those moments when you were here with me. I always wanted to tell you how much you mean to me. My life is in a vegetative state without you in it. I do not know what binds us together, but whatever it is, it is blessed by the Gods. I love you more than I thought I ever could, and I ever will. You are my eternity."

She wiped her tears, and before she could gather her breath to answer, he whispered, "I love you, Riya."

Riya wakes up in a daze and looks around. Her pillow was wet from the tears that were still there, soaking her cheeks. The dream felt surreal. She could feel every ounce of emotion that dripped from his voice. She rubs her hand, not quite believing that the goosebumps she has were just because of a conversation she dreamt.

Oh, if only love like this ~~exists~~ lasts.
Magari!

Chapter 1

Barrett Park, Boothbay Harbor, Maine.
16th April 2019

"Papa, that lady's scarf is so pretty." Anaya pointed towards a woman engrossed in reading at the far end of the beach.

Sam was walking down the boardwalk with his eleven-year-old daughter Anaya. He loved coming to the beach and watching the waves. He could never stop being fascinated as they swarmed in and instantly receded, leaving traces behind. Just like memories, adulthood, and life, as such!

But today, he was lost in random thoughts dancing in his mind in Brownian motion. He couldn't make out any pattern, but he knew that they were causing chaos, poking every nook and corner of his mind.

He was pondering over how his life is similar to these crashing waves. One moment everything feels like heading in the right direction, achieving heights, and just the next moment, life loses its vigor, and the highs recede, leaving behind the traces of memories. *Memories!* Memories which you can either cherish and smile or step on to its shards and bleed with the pain.

"Mm-hmm. Let's change into our swimming gear, honey." He had been distracted today, not knowing why.

He knew that he rarely got to spend time with his daughter, and still, he was not present with her completely.

What's bothering me? he thought to himself.

Looking at the tiniest speck of foam that danced on the waves, he related his existence to that drop of foam clinging on to the waves of life, trying to survive the uncertainties.

He couldn't quite place the feelings that were causing turmoil in his heart. In the morning, he had woken up to a strange dream, in which he was begging someone to come back to him. Even in the dream, he could feel he was insanely in love with this person. His voice felt like the way it used to be during his college times, spilling words of endearment and promises of the future. *Love! Gone are those days of purity.* He had woken up with goosebumps, making him laugh. He rarely had dreams and couldn't believe it could have such a physiological effect on him.

Since morning he had tried to busy himself with regular chores, but something was bothering his gut. It was one of those days when you are lost in your thoughts which were not even concretely present. He had nothing in his mind to think, yet he was lost in the volcano of thoughts, almost at the edge of erupting.

"And she looks Indian." Sam was suddenly pulled out from his sea of thoughts. He looked at Anaya with adoration. All these years, she had been his anchor to reality. She was eleven, but her maturity always bowled him over.

She was born in India. They had moved to the U.S. when she was just one-year-old. Even after ten years of being in the U.S., she still had a deep fascination with every Indian she saw. And her fascination kept growing as the U.S. flooded with Indians of all kinds.

Apparently, adults make peace with new nationalities and cultures. We blend into the culture and adapt to their ways of living with the fear of standing out. We get so busy making a living that we hardly pay attention to the culture we leave behind. The new place, the new culture, and contemporary society gets profoundly engraved in our personalities that we hardly can distinguish between the two. But as for the kids, there is always a sense of belongingness. They hold on to a place with something more than just roots. They connect with a sense that is beyond geographical boundaries. And we say that children are fickle-minded. *Believe me, the irony is not lost on me.*

"Dad! Where are you lost?" Anaya pulled Sam's hand, jerking a speck of his consciousness to the present.

"Nowhere. Let's change and go for a swim." He bent down to kiss her.

"No. Let's go and talk to her." Anaya started pulling Sam by his hand, pointing towards the lady who just gulped down her beer.

"Anaya! You cannot just go and talk to every Indian you see."

"Why not?" Anaya asked, folding her hands as if there was no logical sense to what her dad just said.

"Because," Sam stopped midway, "You…"

What Sam? Why can't she? he thought to himself.

Sam wished if he could just see the face of this lady and maybe judge if she would mind a restless eleven-year-old ruining her pleasant afternoon. His mind was once again wandering aimlessly in a desert of parched thoughts.

Adulthood is not fun, except for the fact that we don't have to ask for our parent's permission to visit our friends, but the rest is like plain yogurt, without any flavor. We sometimes get over absorbed in adulting that we end up taking life too seriously. We stop questioning why we resist simple actions. He had no answer to Anaya's question, nor he even questioned why they can't go and talk to an Indian who is merely enjoying the beach. Most of the time, we are all so conscious of being an adult that we fail to take pleasure in introducing ourselves to strangers, just for the sake of greetings.

Don't we all crave human connection? Even if it lasts for just a moment. But surprisingly, we take adulting, which, by the way, we dislike so much in all earnestness and turn the personal boundaries into walls, failing to acknowledge the presence of another breathing heart. Even saying a simple *hello* requires us to step outside our comfort zone.

Had it been any other day, Sam would have made an effort for Anaya and talked to whomever she wanted. But today, something wasn't working inside his brain, and he just wanted to take a dip in the cold water and drown his thoughts or whatever that were doing acrobatics in his head.

"Let's swim first. Then we can go have a chat with her. Ok?"

Anaya looked skeptically at him but agreed.

It is strange how kids trust adults easily and believe in their promises, unaware of the fact that adults themselves neither trust nor believe in their own promises. They cannot accept the fact that a string of words is capable of binding them into something that may demand them to move out of their comfort zone. Continually being thrown out of comfort zones through the highs and lows of teenage and college life, adults are suckers for those!

Sam held her hand, and they headed towards the bathrooms to change.

Chapter 2

Barrett Park, Boothbay Harbor, Maine
16th April 2019

Riya was sitting on her beach chair, with feet comfortably dug in the sand and reading. Her eyes had started to tire as she had been reading since morning. The sun had moved places, and she was still exploring the snow-covered cobbled streets of Rye. She remembered what her eye doctor had told her. She realized her eyes hurt because she loses track of time when reading, and the movement of her eyes is limited since she doesn't let them rest.

Downing the last pint of beer, she kept the book in her lap and looked around at nothing in particular.

There were a couple of families with kids in their cute bathing suits, a few joggers, and some baby boomers strolling around, probably reminiscing the time when they also used to run. The beach was filled with half-naked people running around and trying to have the time of their lives. She suddenly thought to herself how body shaming somehow ceases to exist on the beaches.

It has been nine years now that Riya has been staying in Boothbay Harbor, a small art town in Maine.

She disliked coming to the beach during the spring breaks since it was overrun with people on their way to

Acadia National Park, and it was harder to find quiet and peace. But today, she wanted to escape the dream she had and the remnants of feelings that still made her shiver. So, she had come in early today to read and was happy to find a quiet spot across the boardwalk. It was taking every bit of her effort to keep that dream at bay.

But the thing about reading and drinking beer at the beach is that no matter how relaxed you feel, you have to spend half your time running over to the restrooms. And during this time, when the spring breaks are in full swing, people arrive in swarms and almost make it impossible to find a clean restroom.

So, for the 8th time in the past 3 hours, Riya lifted her lazy butt and headed to the restroom.

"Hey, you are the lady with the pretty scarf." The voice startled her.

"Oh?" Riya turned around to see a little girl in a blue swimsuit with small unicorns all over it.

"We saw you from across the boardwalk. I love your scarf."

Riya smiled at the little girl who was looking brightly at the tassels of her scarf. She realized how easy it is for the kids to speak their minds and compliment people.

"Thanks, sweetheart. I love your cute little clip." She dried her hands and turned to look at her.

"My dad bought it for me on Valentine's day." She adorned it proudly.

"Valentine's day! It seems like your dad loves you a lot." Riya loved being around kids. She always felt a sense of calm whenever she was with them. And surprisingly, she had a knack for making kids adore her. She knew how to talk to them, which most adults, even the parents themselves, don't know.

"Of course. He says I am the prettiest girl in the whole world."

Riya laughed.

"What's your name, pretty girl with a cute clip?"

"Anaya."

"Wow, that's a beautiful name. What does that mean?"

She thought before speaking, and her eyes twinkled as she explained, "Papa says it is from the Hebrew language. It means 'answer of God.'"

"Wow! Your dad must be immensely proud of you."

"Yes. He says when I was born, all his questions were answered. I don't know what that means. But can I tell you a secret?" Anaya's eyes twinkled with the thrill that came with breaking rules.

"Ooh! I love secrets!" Riya shared her excitement with equal thrill.

"Papa told me he was failing his exams because he didn't know any answers. And when I was born, he excelled in all his exams and stood first."

Riya laughed at the naive innocence of this little girl. She suddenly had a feeling that her father must be a really cool person to have it explained to his daughter in such a way.

"It looks like you helped your papa cheat," Riya said mischievously.

She giggled. "Where did you get the scarf from?" Anaya asked, playing with the tassels.

"Do you want it?"

Anaya nodded in excitement.

"Here, take it." Riya removed it from her neck and tied it around Anaya.

"Really?" Anaya was ecstatic.

It is so easy to make kids happy, she thought to herself.

"It looks prettier on you." Riya smiled at her.

"Thank you so much. You are awesome!"

Suddenly Riya's phone started ringing.

"Riya! Where the hell are you?" Someone yelled from the other side of the phone.

"Hi, Aarush," Riya said patiently as if to convey to him that there is niceness in courtesies.

"Arghh, get over your courtesies! I am waiting for you at the cafe." Aarush exhaled impatiently.

"Be right there."

"Ok, Anaya, I have to go. It was a pleasure meeting you. Enjoy your stay." Riya waved her goodbye and left.

Chapter 3

Blue Moon Cafe, Boothbay Harbor, Maine
16th April 2019

"There you are. Finally!" Aarush looked over from his iPad and got up to hug Riya. His blue jeans with a half-tugged white shirt and the unruly hair were enough to turn a couple of heads towards him.

"Who died?" Riya asked, rolling her eyes. She had known Aarush for over seven years now, and he was one of the closest persons to Riya. It was only because of Aarush that her life's usually well-settled routine was trampled upon and turned into chaos. She enjoyed sailing in this chaos once every little while.

"Come on! I am leaving in two days. Wait! Were you at the beach, reading again?" Aarush said, snatching the copy of 'The Invention of Wings' poking from her bag.

"What do you have against my reading at the beach?" She tried to grab her book only to hit her knee by the table. Exasperated, she sat down and picked the menu.

"I have nothing against reading or the beach per se, but definitely against reading at the beach. It's blasphemous!" Aarush said, enjoying her frustration. He never enjoyed annoying anyone more than Riya. He loved how she got flustered and made faces. She was a potpourri of animated expressions.

"Did you just learn that word and are trying to use it in a sentence?"

"Reese! You know what I mean."

"Don't call me that!"

A waiter appeared with their coffee and brunch.

"I already ordered your coffee and food. I am famished." Aarush took away the menu from her and handed it to the waiter.

"Looks like you haven't gone home yet?" She raised her eyes.

"You know mom! She will be freaked out if I tell her that her son is leaving again in two days." Aarush poured her coffee and took a bite of Cinnabon muffin.

"She will know, Aarush."

"Not unless you tell her."

"She sees right through me. She knew the last time too when you didn't go home, and we met at your place."

"That's your fault, not mine. Your face gives away too much. Don't you know girls should be subtle? That's why you are single."

"Shut up, Aarush." She threw a napkin at him.

"Ok, ok. Back to your reading on the beach. You are literally disrespecting the beach, Reese."

"Disrespecting? Are you even making sense?"

"Reese! Beach is meant to chill and drown in those calm, clear waters. Have you forgotten my mantra?" he continues taking a sip of his coffee, "Do not take life too seriously."

"It's not worth the faith you put in it!" Riya says along, mimicking him. Aarush beamed his charming smile. He was an irony in himself. He was one of the most casual and carefree people she ever met. It took her almost a year to understand that beneath all the flirting and fun that Aarush did, he was a warm and caring person and had a deep passion for things he really wanted in life.

"I drown myself in words and literature." Riya had the habit of picking a word from people's sentences and giving it back to them, especially if it was Aarush.

"Aaah! I knew something was fundamentally wrong with you ever since I saw you."

"And still, you followed me from India to the U.S."

"If that thought makes your single, tragic life tolerable, be my guest!" Aarush laughed at her. They have been the best of friends for years now, and their day never ended without their friendly banter. Aarush traveled frequently, and they never missed a chance to have fun with each other whenever he was around.

"Anyway, where are you off to now?"

"Cuba!"

"Wow! Colorful cars." Riya called out to the waiter for the cheque.

"See! I don't understand what you read about so much. Such superficial knowledge! Cuba, Reese, is not just colorful cars. It is a land of mixed culture and a well-preserved society. Their culture is amongst the richest ones."

"Ok, ok. Don't give me your historical cultures lecture."

"That's the only way I guess you will ever travel the world." Aarush shook his head.

"Such an obnoxious creature you are. Anyway, for how long are you gone this time?"

"Why? Will you miss me?" He grinned. Despite being close to each other, Aarush never missed a chance to tease and flirt with Riya.

"Ya right! The best days of my life are when I don't have to tolerate your annoying face with that unkempt hair. Wash it, Aarush!"

"This is a total chick magnet! Just look around!" He said, spreading his arms. "What would you know anyway? You are a dry land when it comes to men." Aarush flicked his hair, and they laughed. "Anyway, I am having a party at my place tomorrow. Help me with the food."

"Am I invited?" Riya always loved the parties that Aarush organized. They were a mix of all kinds of people, and she always felt thrilled to know about their journeys.

"Of course. Otherwise, who will get drunk and entertain my guests."

"You…" Riya got up from her chair and punched his shoulder.

"On a serious note, I have something important to tell you," Aarush said a little seriously.

"Serious?" Riya raised her eyebrows. Aarush nods solemnly, "Let's go!" He started walking ahead without waiting for her knowing well that she will catch up.

Chapter 4

Riya was smiling all her way back. The mere presence of Aarush was enough to bring vibrance to her life. She waved and greeted a few people while walking down the lane leading to her home. When Riya reached home, her neighbor, Mrs. Jennie, called out to her.

"Did you meet Aarush?"

Riya hesitated a bit but gave up. "How do you always know?"

Mrs. Jennie just smiled at her without replying.

"Yes, I met with him." Suddenly she remembered why he invited her to the party, "He is a jerk."

"You guys fought again?"

"Fought? Who fights with him? He is not worth my energy."

Mrs. Jennie smiled at her.

They had been neighbors for nine years. Riya had shifted here from Portland after finishing her one-year certificate course in Architecture. Over the past few years, after Mrs. Jennie's husband passed away and her kids got busy with their lives, she had come to adore Riya more. They had started with sharing evening teas. And over the years, along with the tea and cakes, Mrs. Jennie loved baking; they have shared their feelings, emotions, and life in all.

"You have fought like Tom & Jerry all these years. I have no idea what keeps you both going. I was afraid only one of you would survive your sarcasm wars." Mrs. Jennie said, turning the soil over in one of the pots.

"He invited me to his place to prepare food for a party tomorrow. Can you believe that jerk?" She said, throwing her bag on the chair and helping Mrs. Jennie turn the soil in other pots.

"It is your fault. Why did you let him eat with you all those years when he used to return from exotic lands with inedible food?" Mrs. Jennie knew all the people Riya had ever been close to. She had been the sunshine of her days. They had spent so many summer days sitting on the front porch sharing a laugh over something that either of them was reading. Mrs. Jennie was like a book full of wisdom, whose grammar was made out of fun and wit.

"I didn't know he would never grow up. He is an asshole." Mrs. Jennie laughed as Riya started plucking the weeds out from the pots.

Chapter 5

"Aarush, I am not going grocery shopping alone for your party," Riya called Aarush on her way to the nearby deli store.

"But Reese, I am busy with preparing my R.V. for the next trip."

"I hate you. By the way, what's the status of mine?"

"It should be ready soon. I have done my part. Now I have asked a friend of mine to fix the sliders of the shelves. I have no idea from where you designed it all."

"I studied Architecture. Remember?"

"You survived Architecture. Remember?"

"Jerk! And I hope you mentioned him about the opening patio too."

"Why do you need it anyway? It's causing so much trouble with the assembly."

"Aarush!"

"Ya ya! I get it. Your book-cafe on wheels. Wouldn't it be so pathetically lonely?"

"Don't worry. I won't barge in your exotic adventures."

"You need help!" She could feel Aarush rolling his eyes.

"Of course! So, come and pick these damn grocery bags, else I am going home, and you can serve mac & cheese to your guests."

"Fine! You are bloody demanding. Be right there."

Aarush picked Riya along with the grocery bags. Riya had always been a sensational cook. She loved experimenting with food, and Aarush's friends always enjoyed the sumptuous meals cooked by her at his parties. Riya knew most of his friends, although he would have some new additions that he met during his countless travels every time.

Riya suddenly turned excitedly towards Aarush. "Hey, is Liam coming?"

"Reese! Get over him already!"

"What? He is so dreamy!"

"You just like his name. Nothing else."

"So what? It's such a dip-a-brownie-in-chocolate-sauce delicious name."

Aarush looked at Riya with pity.

"Enough with that look. Is he coming?" She tried to remove the strand of hair dancing in front of her eyes. Aarush looked at her and rolled his eyes.

"You know, someday your eyes will roll back to your brain."

"Why the hell do you have to keep your hair open when you know it's difficult to manage when you have grocery bags to hold?" He turned towards her and placed the strand of hair behind her ear.

"Because it's party time, with Liam. So, is he coming?"

"Yes. And that Irish wuss also asked if you will be there."

"Aah! Don't be jealous, my munchkin." Riya tried being cute and held his cheeks. He shrugged her off.

"Don't be cute with me. Have you forgotten the ruckus you created last time? Anyway, just don't drink too much. I almost had to see you making out with that poor Liam last time."

"Don't!" Riya turned towards him sharply and locked his lips together with her fingers. "I told you."

"Ya ya! I am not bringing it up again. Why do you bother to drink when you have such a low tolerance for alcohol? It works well for me, though. Drunk Riya is so much fun."

"Jerk!"

They reached Aarush's studio apartment. It was more of a small room that had a huge open terrace. One of the giant walls had a huge, life-size world map, with several scribbled notes on the countries he had visited or was yet to visit. He had been traveling ever since Riya had known him. She thought that he would be exhausted after some time, but the zeal with which Aarush traveled and worked was something Riya couldn't comprehend. She needed the feeling of belongingness and a sense of security, unlike Aarush. She was always fascinated by Aarush's travel stories and this wall of experiences that seemed too foreign to Riya.

Aarush carried the grocery bags and kept them on the kitchen counter. He played songs on the speaker and gestured Riya to take the floor.

"Am I done? Your Bollywood songs are playing; the veggies are here; you know where the knives are, and here is your wine. Now I'll get the hell out of your way before you get all bitchy." Aarush said, ticking off the list mentally.

"Good to know you remember the drill, especially of getting the hell out of my way!" Riya wrapped the apron and kicked it off.

"I do not want another bleeding nose." They both laughed at the memory of four years back. Riya was preparing a meal at her place, and Aarush was trying to talk to her. He kept coming towards the kitchen platform, sometimes to refill his drink or snacks or just to keep the glass in the sink. Riya was so frustrated with the constant disturbance that she flew her arms in frustration, which hit Aarush's nose. And Aarush bruised like a peach. "Why the hell were you coming in my way? I told you to get the hell out of the kitchen." These were the exact words she used while bandaging his nose.

Learning from his mistakes and Riya's temper, Aarush went to the backyard and got busy with the R.V. while Riya absorbed herself in the aromas of oils and spices.

Chapter 6

"Aarush, just switch off the left stove after 5 minutes. I am going to change." Riya called out to Aarush.

"You are changing? Please don't clean the bathroom, like the last time. I want things at arm's length and not on the shelves where they almost disappear."

"Live like a human at least when you are home."

Aarush waved her off and screwed the last few pieces that were left in place. He came upstairs to a luscious aroma. He was about to peep in the dishes when Riya yelled from the washroom. "Don't you dare open the covers of the dishes! You will spoil the taste."

Aarush rolled his eyes unconsciously, "Dammit! My eyes may actually roll back to my brain." He took out his clothes from his wardrobe as Riya emerged with a hint of musk, dressed in a cherry printed frock.

"Do I look like someone an Irish guy might be interested in?" She had applied lip gloss and eyeliner. She was never a makeup person.

Aarush smiled at her and flicked her head. "You look as fresh as a dewdrop."

Riya raised her eyebrows at his compliments.

"Reese! Red or blue?" Aarush held up two shirts.

"Blue checks! And please iron it." Aarush rolled his eyes again exasperatedly and took out the iron board.

The party started around 8 pm, and Liam was one of the first few guests to arrive. As he entered, Aarush raised an eye towards Riya, talking to a girl from Vietnam, who was here as an exchange dance student. Riya caught his glance and blushed.

She had met Liam at Aarush's New year's party last year, and they had instantly hit off. Aarush was precise in commenting that she loved the sound of his name more than the guy himself. But these parties were like cheat days for Riya when she dropped all her inhibitions and had pure fun. *Moreover, he has such long fingers.* Riya shook her head and blushed at her thoughts as Liam caught her eyes and bowed his head a little in acknowledgment.

As the party progressed, drinks were served, and the food was relished. Everybody appreciated Riya for her amazingly delectable preparations. As the party took its full form, everybody started cheering for Riya and Aarush to dance.

"May I?" Aarush came towards Riya and offered his hand.

"What a fake gentleman." Riya laughed and accepted his hand.

He rolled her over swiftly as she pressed against his chest. They looked at each other and went seven years back when they had first met while dancing.

"Remember?" Aarush whispered in her ear.

They smiled at each other with years of familiarity and comfort. The music picked up beats as they grooved and turned oblivious to the audience. Their feet were as happy as their hearts.

One thing that kept them strong was their love for dance. They both were the happiest when they danced. They knew each other's moves and were comfortable in each other's arms while they hustled. An aura of warmth radiated from them when they moved together to the rhythm. Their smiles widened, and their feet swayed with ecstasy.

Aarush rolled her over again and let her perform solo. He knew how much she loved the attention she got when she danced. Riya was flawless when it came to dancing. He looked at her with a proud feeling. Her eyes radiated a sense of being when she sailed through the space around her. It was like she was in a state of trance. All her inhibitions came loose when she let her feet do the talking. It was as if she was high on music. And before she tumbled after being absorbed in all the highs, Aarush caught her at the perfect beat.

As the song ended, they bowed to everyone with jubilant smiles.

Liam approached Riya with a glass of wine. She was down three pints of beer and knew she shouldn't be drinking more. Moreover, Riya was well aware she shouldn't be mixing the drinks. But she couldn't escape the sexy accent with which Liam offered her the wine. She took the glass from his hand, and they headed to the edge of the terrace.

Liam brushed a strand of hair from her face while looking deep into her eyes.

"Your eyes are an ocean of intensity." He whispered in his Irish accent that had drowned her last time.

"I hope you know how to swim." Riya tilted her glass towards Liam and locked her eyes with his.

"I wish I didn't. I would love to drown in them." Liam rubbed her cheeks tenderly. They heard people clapping and dancing. As they turned around, the music had changed, and a few of Aarush's friends were dancing.

She spotted Aarush standing with a Korean guy, laughing at something.

"Can I have the pleasure to dance with you?" Liam bent with his hand towards Riya. Riya took his hand, and they headed towards the music. She noticed Aarush straightening his back and looking at her amused.

Liam rolled her around and held her by her waist. They started moving slowly as Liam's palms rested on her back. Riya could feel his fingers moving over the silk of her dress. They slowly started to move up as he pulled Riya a little closer to his face. This was definitely not the kind of dancing Riya was comfortable with. *Or maybe it was the person she was dancing with.*

Aarush noticed the change in Riya's demeanor. He shook his head and threw his beer bottle in the trash. He quietly changed the track and headed to where Liam and Riya were dancing. He patted Liam's shoulder and smiled. He could see the relief in Riya's eyes.

"I need her for some food emergency." He took Riya's hand and pulled her to a corner.

"How drunk are you?" asked Aarush.

"Drunk enough to notice that you are a little pissed," Riya said cautiously, knowing that she may have angered Aarush as he had warned her not to drink more than she could handle.

"Reese!"

"Why do you call me that? Learn from Liam. He rolls his tongue when he says my name. It is so sexy." She tried to take a sip from her glass when Aarush pulled it out from her grasp.

"Reese! Enough of drinking! Why the hell are you drinking wine? I saw you had a beer."

"Liam offered." She said as a matter of fact with a smile as big as her face could hold.

"So, am I the only person you can refuse? Can't you say no to him!" Aarush hissed.

"He was just being nice," Riya said slowly, dropping her cheerfulness, aware of the heat that radiated from Aarush's body because of his anger.

"Yeah, too much nice." Aarush moved his hand through his hair in distinct annoyance.

"Aww. Don't be so insecure. You know you are the best."

"Fine, then let me call him only. Let his finger also do the talking." He took a step away, and Riya immediately grabbed his hands and looked at him with puppy eyes.

"Ok, ok. Sorry." said Riya, visibly embarrassed, still holding his hands and playing with his fingers.

"Reese!" Aarush said affectionately, turning towards her. His shoulders slumped as his anger dissipated, and his tone suddenly became warm as if he could cradle this delicate person standing next to him. He knew he could never be angry with Riya for more than a few minutes. He had this innate desire to protect her and make sure that absolutely nothing and no one ever hurt her.

"Sometimes it just feels good, Aarush, to feel that you are loved," Riya whispered, still looking down at their entangled hands.

Aarush bent his face down to hers and rubbed her cheeks with his thumb.

"That's not love, Reese. And you know it better than I do."

"At least it makes you feel that someone likes you. And that you aren't alone in this world."

Aarush released his hands from hers and cupped her face with both his palms.

"Reese! You are never alone. You always have me. And you know that!"

Riya snorted. "Liam thinks my eyes are exquisite. You, on the other hand, always fight and tease me. He makes me feel beautiful."

Aarush held her face and made her look at him. He looked deep into her eyes. Riya tried to fight him away, but he held her tighter.

"Reese! You are the most beautiful person I have ever met in my life. I have traveled a great deal, and there is absolutely no one who even compares to you. He is right indeed! Your eyes hold oceans of emotions, but the depth scares me. Your innocence and purity worry me. It's so easy to hurt you. You are too precious, Reese. You are too precious for this world. And no matter what, Reese, I am always there for you. I am your little world, and I am never gonna let anyone cause you even the slightest bit of sorrow."

"Where did you learn this speech from?"

Aarush chuckled and gave her a warm hug. He wiped off tears from her face and took her inside. He gave her a bowl of pasta and ordered her to eat.

"How can you forget to eat your own cooked food? That's why you get high. You are such a teenager. Just drinks and no food!"

Aarush shook his head as he took a spoonful of pasta and offered it to Riya. She was a little sober after eating. Aarush gave her a glass of cold water and flicked her forehead. "Idiot!"

As the night descended and the moon shifted its position, the party thinned. Liam kissed Riya goodbye. The few remaining friends helped Aarush clean the house and throw the trash. Riya changed to her regular clothes as everyone left, took a rug, and spread it on the terrace, overlooking the town. Aarush came with a pint and sat with her.

Riya raised her eyes as he offered her a pint.

"I know how to handle you."

"Are you still mad?"

Aarush just gave her a look and looked at the twinkling lights coming from the town.

"You only said you wanted entertainment. You knew what happens when I am drunk. Weren't you looking forward to it?"

Aarush let out a sigh and turned towards Riya. "Reese! I am worried about you. You can go kiss anyone you want, but at least be sincere about it. I know you would have regretted tomorrow morning. I have known you enough to know how bloody morally straight you are."

"I am sorry."

"Are you ok? Why don't you join me on this trip? You will enjoy it."

"Enjoy what? Shitting on the ground and wet bedsheets!"

"That happened just once. It's not even monsoon yet."

"Ya ya. What will happen to all those adventures you have with those hippie girls? Hey, what happened to that girl from Bali?"

"Don't even remind me of her. I would have been in jail had it not been my instinct to run away when she offered her 'services' while rolling that joint. If you know what I mean."

"I always know what you mean, Aarush."

"And moreover, you know I have come a long way from those times. You are aware of my sincerity now. You know where my heart resides."

"You have come a long way Aarush, both personally and professionally, from looking for investors for your idea to expanding your ideas all over the world."

"And you laughed at my idea."

"I was never a good judge of character, I guess," Riya said with a tinge of melancholy.

"Reese!" Aarush said warmly as he pulled her closer. They both were lying on the rug and facing the sky.

"I am fine, Aarush. Just tend to get a bit lonely sometimes."

"Reese! You need to let go of your past. You carry it everywhere, but it makes you lonelier."

Aarush looked at her somberly. When Riya didn't say anything, he lifted her hand he was holding and kissed it affectionately. "You know I am always there for you."

Riya nodded and smiled at him.

"Of course! Life can't be that easy! I have to deal with a jerk like you."

Aarush laughed along with her, and they lay there absorbing the vastness of the sky.

Chapter 7

After spending the morning and half of the afternoon on the beach, Riya was dehydrated from the humidity. The hangover from the last night further contributed to it. Aarush was supposed to meet her before leaving for Cuba. She walked over to the nearest Starbucks for A.C. and ordered a coffee. She never really liked coming to Starbucks because of all the pretentious people who savored the overpriced coffee that tasted the same as any nearby cafe.

Suddenly, she heard a familiar voice.

"Oh! Hi, the lady with the pretty scarf."

"Hey! Hi! Anaya, right?" Anaya chirped as Riya remembered her name. She noticed that Anaya was wearing her scarf. "Well, right now, you are the one with the pretty scarf."

Anaya giggled.

"Where is your dad? It is so crowded here. You should not be alone."

Anaya pointed to her dad, who was in the line for the order. Riya could only see his back, and by the way he was standing, she could sense he was flustered with the rush around. *Not a Starbucks fan either*, she thought to herself and smiled.

We, humans, are community-oriented people. The moment we find someone with the same nooks and cranny as us, we form a community in our heads; a mental community. It's like showing solidarity over others who like what you don't. You also don't like Starbucks? Great. You also prefer tea over coffee? Perfect. You also have never seen Game of Thrones? Awesome, me neither. And it goes on forever.

"You should go stand with him. My coffee should be ready."

Anaya walks towards the cashier as Riya makes her way towards the next pick-up counter.

"Pa, look whom I found! The lady with the pretty scarf."

"Sam. Donuts and coffee," Sam said, placing his order. He hated coming to Starbucks. The unnecessary hype, the rush; people trying to look busy, tapping on their keyboards, reading a classic they may not even understand, all the while sipping overly priced coffees.

"Wait, wait. Lemme get our donuts." He held her hand and moved to the next counter. "And did you ask her name this time?"

Just then, a barista called out for Riya's order in a loud voice to make sure the customer hears amidst the noise and placed her order on the counter along with several others.

"Riya!"

Sam stopped breathing for a while, hearing the familiar name. It is strange how certain names hold all our precious feelings and how whenever you hear that name, your entire sanity goes berserk.

He took a deep breath and let the feeling of the name pass by. He turned towards the counter to look for his order when his eyes confronted his past.

"Sameer." Riya mouthed the name, scared that it would break under the overwhelming feelings.

The chaos around them settled into a murmur, and a beating silence surfaced. The only sound was of their heart beating wildly as if exposed after being caged for decades.

Years of silence!

Years of words left unsaid. If words could create a space of silence, this would be it.

Their vision blurred as tears rolled from their eyes, without asking permission from their owners.

Chapter 8

The absence of twelve years was a long one to give words to. It was like you are deep down in a sea of memories, where all you can hear is the sound of your own breath and the splashes of nostalgia that hits you. You fail to even feel the tears that give away your facade.

Meanwhile, a customer from behind yelled at Sam for holding up the line. It took efforts for Sam to merge with reality. He realized that those eyes looking deep inside him were rolling tears. He took a step forward to wipe those off and stopped midway. Some habits never change. They were like a reflex.

"Come sit with us, Riya." Anaya came around, unaware of how the world just changed for them. Unaware of the cornucopia of feelings that were being exchanged.

"I... I need to go, Anaya. I have a..." Riya was so overwhelmed that she couldn't find her own voice, or the conviction for anything other than the person standing in front of her was really Sameer, *her Sameer!*

"No-No. Look, it's raining. Your coffee will spoil." She started pulling Riya towards the corner seat, unaware of the fact that her eyes were still locked with Sameer, who was cemented at his spot.

Before Riya could argue, Anaya pulled her to the seat. It was the kind of awkwardness that exists between the two people who had known each other to the core of their souls but were practically strangers now.

Anaya got busy looking at the strokes of brushes on her scarf. The two strangers were still trying to absorb their rich past in the present. Sam couldn't believe his eyes. He couldn't believe he was sitting with Riya, *her Riya, after twelve years!* He couldn't comprehend that God would make this happen. He had put a curtain over his past and had divided his life into 'before' and 'after'. The 'before' always trying to move into the 'after' but continuously being pushed back.

It is strange how you use the phrase 'finding the long-lost person' when you meet someone after years of absence. It's like finding your old diary, which was lost in all the chaos of growing up, in precisely the same state as you left it, making you feel just the same, except with a tinge of sadness at the things lost.

He couldn't find words that could do justice to this moment. He kept looking at Riya, who was nervously digging her fingers, not knowing what to do with the reality that the present had thrown at them.

"She really likes your scarf. She wears it everywhere she goes." Sam tries to speak slowly and cautiously as if scared to disperse this moment.

Hearing his voice, the veneer of living life was destroyed. It felt as if she had been holding her breath for years, and his voice loosened the threads. She had always been intoxicated by his voice. They had survived a long-distance relationship, and she always felt that she was in a relationship with his voice. Within a second of hearing his voice, she could understand what he was feeling at the other end of the phone. Hearing his voice again after so long laid her heart bare to all the emotions she had locked up in a safe place inside her heart.

"Yes. It smells like Pa but in a girly way. If that's possible." They were startled to hear Anaya's voice. Somehow, they felt as if there were just the two of them. "Do you also use musk?" Anaya asked, looking innocently at Riya.

Riya coughed as her breath got stuck while escaping the emotions.

Sameer's eyes were searching for hers. *So, she uses my perfume even now, after years.* As she lifted her eyes, she noticed Sameer looking at her. The feeling of opia washed over them. The depth of vulnerability and emotion that passed between their eyes was startling, raw, and almost unsettling in its familiarity. There were years of restlessness that danced between them. The words were desperate to spill but were blocked by a transparent barrier. They were trying to squirt, pushing across the boundary, but were somehow being held back.

It felt like the moment of a lifetime.

Riya had associated every feeling with Sameer. Without him, she was as barren as the death-valley. Riya gathered her strength and looked away. She knew that the longer she sat across Sam, the more difficult it would be to keep a hold of reality.

It had stopped raining, and people had started to leave. Suddenly Aarush appeared from nowhere, kept his hand around her shoulder, and crushed her under his weight.

"There you are! How do you find such secluded places everywhere? Come, let's hurry."

Looking at how awkward Riya was, he looked at her. Riya swallowed a lump and pointed towards Sam.

"Umm... Aarush, he is…"

Before Riya could complete, Aarush shook Sam's hand.

"Sorry, bro. This nerd is all about courtesies. It drives me insane. Reese! We don't have time. Let's hurry."

She stumbled along and spilled someone's coffee as she left in a hurry, Sameer's eyes never leaving hers. She couldn't understand how a heart could be so numb yet full of emotion at the same time. Her heartbeat felt like the entangled reel of old cassette tapes.

Riya's Diary
23rd December 2016

Sameer

It is after really long I am writing to you. It's not like I have stopped remembering you, but I have somehow accepted the way it is. It is impossible to separate your existence from mine. Because every little thing that I do is somehow amalgamated with your absence. I always believed in the strength of our bond, but I never thought that the same strength would overpower me when it came to live a life without you.

Yesterday I went to drop off a friend at the airport. You know how I am a sucker for airport hugs and kisses. Aren't those the purest? I know, I know we have discussed this so much already. But come on, isn't it ironic that a place that is as public as an airport witnesses the most intimate feelings and emotions? Never mind!

So, when I was coming back from the airport, I got off at this French place I really love. I was sipping my coffee and looking at people passing by. (Yes! The way I always do! You should also try doing that, rather than being envious of the fact that despite being with you, I am more interested in other people's life.) Anyway, like always, my thoughts started overflowing.

Surprisingly, my imaginative mind drifted to the day we'll meet again. I have never let my mind drift towards this thought ever. Because accepting the fact that you aren't in my life anymore was one of the hardest things I had to do. And I know if I had to do it again, I'll give up. That is why I was surprised at my own thoughts.

I imagined myself sitting at this very own cafe, and due to my habit of being highly perceptive of my surroundings, I am keenly aware of a familiar voice. I get back to my reading, and suddenly the voice is coming from somewhere opposite my table. I look up from my book, and I am astonished! It's you! You are talking to someone on the phone and don't notice me sitting across you, because let's face it, you hardly look around and just focus on your food. I call out your name with glee, and I can see that spark of recognition in your eyes. We both hug each other tightly. We utter some gibberish and hug again, tighter. It's like we were trying to squeeze in all the years we have missed being with each other.

We looked so elated. We have tears of happiness in our eyes. We hug again for a little longer and let our tears flow free. You look at me and wipe my tears as you have always done, and we giggle. You hug me again and whisper, "I have missed you." And I knew that would be enough to melt me in your presence.

Will we ever meet again, Sameer?

Will all the years of absence evaporate by a simple hug?

Will we feel our hearts again?

Will we hope again?

Chapter 9

She kept walking, not knowing where her feet were taking her. Have you ever dreamt of a moment all your life that, after some point, it blurred the lines separating imagination from reality? You have lived that moment countless times in your head such that you know even the subtle changes in the breath. But when it finally happens, you fail to acknowledge its existence.

How did this happen? She had left her entire life and started a new one.

Sameer? Sameer! Her soul, her life, her essence of being. Sameer!

As she tried to remove hair from her face, she felt tears streaming down.

Sameer!

"Riya. Riya!"

Mrs. Jennie called out to her twice before she snapped to the present.

Riya looked at Mrs. Jennie, feigning recognition. She was taken back to her life twelve years ago, where it was just her and Sameer and the love they shared. Nothing else existed for her then. She was always selfish and deeply consumed when it came to their bond. She had completely lost herself in their love, without any hint of regret at losing touch with the world beyond their love.

"What's wrong, honey?"

"Nothing."

Riya shook her head reflexively. She was nowhere around the reality of the present. She was transported to her life that was far away from the one that she had created here.

"You know your face gives you away. And you cannot fool Mrs. Jennie. Why is your sunny face so gloomy? Did something happen last night?"

"I am ok, Mrs. Jennie. I was at the beach." Not knowing how to even start explaining her feelings, she thought it's better just to let it slide.

"Didn't you enjoy the beach today? I told you not to have high expectations. It's springtime, darling. Of course, visitors will be bustling. You cannot be possessive about places, my love."

Riya tried to smile at Mrs. Jennie. It had been an hour, but Riya was still unable to gather her thoughts. It felt like seeing Sameer's eyes had ripped open her past and the memories had spilled all over the place. And collecting something as delicate as memories was tough. Riya had been doing that ever since she lost Sameer. And it was exhausting.

"I am sure you are not upset over Aarush leaving. Did he say something stupid again? Did something happen yesterday at the party?"

Her mind wandered off to Aarush. She realized that she had no idea when she dropped him off. It was as if that didn't happen. She failed to process the time between being with Sameer and coming home; *if I can still call this home.*

"Come here. I baked a cake. Taste it for me."

Mrs. Jennie went in to get the cake for Riya. She sat on the chair that lay on their common porch where they had spent so many days sipping tea and sharing baking recipes. The place suddenly felt like a stranger to her. She was surprised at her feelings.

"Here." Mrs. Jennie handed the plate to Riya and started preparing tea. "Now tell me what is bothering you?"

She looked at Mrs. Jennie, "Can I ask you something, Mrs. Jennie?"

"Always! It has been pretty long that my experience hasn't been questioned."

She loved this humor about Mrs. Jennie. When everyone was fighting with their age, wanting to stay young, Mrs. Jennie had embraced her old age like vanilla essence in a cake.

"Can something, umm... the place you call home, suddenly feel strange?"

Mrs. Jennie thought about it for a while. She was always a deep thinker, yet she knew never to take life seriously. And that is what made Riya respect her. Riya herself was a deep thinker, but she took life too seriously, which sometimes made her miserable. A profound thinker without a sense of humor is a perfect recipe for disaster.

"Sometimes, this 'something' that you call home may seem like a stranger if it was just a facade to run away from 'something' or 'someone' that used to be your home." She looked at Riya, deep in her thoughts, continuing, "Or in some cases, you may stumble upon that 'someone' you have always called home, and then this 'present something' no longer feels the same. Maybe you really found your home after years of running away and pretending to call 'something else' your home."

She took a long breath and cupped her hands around the warm cup of tea. The breeze turned cooler, and she shivered just slightly. She realized Mrs. Jennie might actually be right. Sameer was her home, her heavenly abode. She had known nothing beyond him as she had gathered all her feelings and emotions and kept it in one person, *Sameer!* But all these years, she had tried to be strong and made this place, Mrs. Jennie, their porch, their evening teas, her home.

She was right. Sometimes you call a place home just because you are scared of being displaced. You are afraid of losing touch with reality. After all, every human being wants to feel belonged.

"Is that a newly painted scarf that you are wearing?"

Riya nodded.

"What happened to the other one that you loved?"

"I gave it to a little girl I met on the beach a few days back," she said absentmindedly.

"Is that why you are lost? Because of the girl?"

"No. Because of the father of that girl." Riya replied as a tear trickled down her cheek, and her eyes met Mrs. Jennie's.

And just by the way Riya spoke, Mrs. Jennie knew. "Oh, my darling." She knew who the father of that girl could be.

Mrs. Jennie had met Riya years back when she came to live next to her home. Riya was young and lost. She spent most of her time reading on the porch outside. She had seen her crying while reading. Other times, Mrs. Jennie saw Riya wandering on the streets, looking at nothing in particular, but lost deeply in her thoughts.

Over the years, she started involving Riya in her life. It started off with their morning ritual of drinking tea. Mrs. Jennie, like Riya, loved drinking tea in the fresh air. That is how they started sharing their lives. Over the span of a few teas, rich books, freshly baked cakes, Mrs. Jennie got to know what brought this young girl to such a small town, far away from her real home.

She had seen Riya gather herself from whatever pieces were left of her heart. In the past few years, she had come to love Riya like her own daughter. And the rest of her smiles were restored by Aarush's annoying presence in her life. She has seen Riya grow around her pain of losing the person she has always been in love with.

And now she understood the torrential rain that might be going within Riya.

She came closer and hugged Riya. She knew that Riya needed warmth more than anything else right now. She needed the security of knowingness, and seeing Sameer might have made her lose her sense of footing, her sense of reality.

Mrs. Jennie released her from her embrace and wiped off her tears she didn't know she still had on her cheeks.

"It was…" she signed in resignation.

Her entire past came knocking on her present's door.

Even after years, she could not give words to the feelings she felt for him. She had so many questions for him. What happened to his marriage? Where was his wife? Why was he here? How has he been? And more importantly, does he still remember her sometimes?

She shook her head to get rid of her thoughts.

"It's ok to have conflicts in your head. It's ok to have questions, darling. Without them, how will you even know what to find an answer for?"

She smiled. Like always, Mrs. Jennie knew what she was thinking. And just like always, her wisdom gave her strength.

"This cake is delicious."

"Does Aarush know?"

Riya shook her head.

Mrs. Jennie gently tucked a strand behind Riya's ear.

"I will leave you to your thoughts. Don't be too harsh on yourself."

Chapter 10

Sameer was in a daze. He hasn't been able to believe the turn his life had just taken. It has been two days since he met Riya. *Riya!* He could still feel her eyes and the way she nervously played with her fingers.

She was so nervous.

Yes, he was also nervous. But he was nervous about giving away what she makes him feel even now, after years. *Why was she nervous?*

Sam, stop thinking!

So that is why the scarf smelled of musk. She still uses my fragrance.

What are you thinking, Sameer? It has been 12 years. Do not even hope about her. She may just like that fragrance.

And who was the guy? Why do I want to kill him and his mile-long smile?

He might be her husband.

But she wasn't wearing a ring.

Is it necessary?

They looked pretty close.

Did you expect her to wait for 12 years even after you married someone else? You lost her!

But her eyes! They were speaking so much. As if she has missed me all these years.

Wishful thinking Sam!

Sameer couldn't stop the flow of thoughts in his head. It was a relief that Anaya had some art assignments, and she was a little busy. He had some time to himself and was lost in Riya's thoughts. He was skiing through the curves and troughs of her memories. He had never expected that he would ever meet her again. He had left Ahmedabad, leaving behind all his memories and entire life. He did try to find Riya, but it seemed like she wasn't ready to be found, at least by him. Despite creating numerous scenarios in his head, he never believed that Riya would someday be right in front of him, let alone with some guy, *who, by the way, was really handsome and charming.*

Anaya came running towards him, breaking his *juska*, and asked him to take her to a store to buy art supplies.

They headed to the nearby store that had a varied selection of art supplies. Sam let Anaya free to explore and take whatever she needed while he waited at the counter, still lost in the reverie.

Chapter 11

Riya was out shopping for her art workshop. It was good that her workshop got an outstanding response this time. It was keeping her mind occupied. It was challenging keeping her thoughts away from Sameer.

Finally, after two days of brooding, she left her home to buy art supplies. She wanted to be sure that she had enough of everything. People were lazy when it came to workshops, so she always provided the supplies and asked people to participate and explore their talent.

To her surprise, she found Anaya looking in the same aisle as her. She was wearing the scarf Riya had given her. Riya suddenly felt conscious. *Sameer would also be here.* Her heart had never been so conflicted for wanting to meet someone yet not being able to face him. She was surprised that even a thought of him being somewhere around gave her heart a reason to flip.

Before Riya could turn her back, Anaya recognized her.

"Hey, Riya," Anaya called out and ran towards her.

"Hi, Anaya. Nice scarf." Riya tried to sound casual.

She giggled.

"Do you also like to paint?"

"Yes. A lot! But why are you…"

Before she could finish, she heard Sameer's voice.

"Anaya. It has been half an…"

Sameer stopped mid-sentence seeing Riya and their eyes locked once again! The feeling was weird. They were lost in each other's eyes yet were conscious of the world around them. For twelve years, they didn't even see each other, and now, in a mere span of three days, they were coincidentally stumbling upon each other in the most alien places. Neither of them knew how to behave or even handle whatever they were feeling.

"Hi." Riya smiled at him cautiously.

"Hey."

"Why are you yelling in a store, Papa. Look who I met again."

Sam smiled at his daughter, who knew nothing about the history her dad shared with Riya.

Both of them stood still, looking at each other, unsure of the correct decorum in such cases.

Breaking the silence, Anaya pulled Sam's hand and said she was hungry and wanted to eat Chinese today.

"Do you like Chinese, Riya?" asked Anaya.

"Me? Yes. Why?"

"Because we are having lunch together. Let's go, Papa."

Before either of them could resist, Anaya pulled them towards the exit. They billed their items and exited.

Chapter 12

They walked towards a small Chinese restaurant with patio seating. As they settled, Riya felt a sense of long-lost familiarity, which she found unable to place.

As they ordered their food and waited for it to arrive, Sam smiled at Anaya's happy face and turned to Riya, who he noticed hadn't said much since they met.

"Is everything ok?"

She nodded, not able to find her voice. *Nothing is ok, Sameer. What are you doing here? I left you along with my life in India. I left you far away. How did you catch up? And why?*

"Do you live nearby?"

"Not really."

"Still love to walk?" He smiled at her.

"Of course. And this place demands to be walked around." Riya cheered up, suddenly finding her voice.

She always got excited when it came to talking about this place. She never looked back since the day she drove here. She had come here for an assignment, which was an escape from reality, and instantly fell in love with the vibe of this place. It took her just one sunset at the beach to call it home.

"Totally your kind of place. I hate to walk around 20 minutes to get a carton of milk."

Riya laughed at him.

Sam looked at her in awe. Her laughter, like long ago, still fills the air around her with blossoming flowers. His tension started to ease as he felt that Riya was getting comfortable.

Despite joking around, Sam was dying to ask her how she had been. A little voice in his heart was desperate to know about the guy who took her off the other day. But he knew he shouldn't be impulsive, or else he may scare her away. Moreover, his heart was still pumping blood at a rate his body couldn't handle.

"How long have you been here?" Sam asked cautiously. He knew that the answer would be the moment that could shut him again out of her life.

Before Riya could answer, their food arrived.

"Sir, here is your order. And these drinks are complimentary. Enjoy your meal."

Papa, give me your phone. This drink looks so lovely. I want to take a picture."

Riya picked her fork and started eating. She somehow had lost her appetite. *So, you still cannot eat when you are with him.* She knew Sameer desperately wanted to know the answer. But that was unchartered territory. She had no idea where she could let this Sameer's train of emotions let go in her space. She didn't want to return to 2007 when Sameer got married and left her broken into millions of pieces that she hasn't been able to collect even now. She had come a long way from losing Sameer to being the girl she is now. She let the aroma of the noodles overtake the conversation, and the moment slipped not really unnoticed but at least uncommitted.

"Riya, do you know how to use chopsticks? I want to learn how to use them."

"I am sorry. I am a fork person. Cannot go through the effort of using chopsticks when the food is in front of me."

"Papa says the same thing. You both are such pigs." She laughed at them.

"Hey!" Sam showed her eyes in anger.

"Sorry, sorry. Do you know once we were at mom's place? She was teaching me how to eat pizza with a fork and knife. She eyed Papa to eat in the same way so that I would follow him and learn." Anaya giggled and looked at Sameer before continuing, "by the time papa finished one slice, everyone had finished their dinner. It was so funny."

Riya noticed Sameer getting a little uncomfortable as Anaya talked about her mom. She wanted to ask if they would be returning to their mom's after having lunch with her but knew she couldn't dare ask the question. It was personal, and she wasn't sure if personal was what she wanted. *But didn't she just say they were at mom's place? Do they not live together? What happened?*

Riya glanced at Sameer, who looked visibly embarrassed, but in an adorable way. She remembered one of the college fests when Sameer visited her, and they were serving pizza on a paper plate. It was those times when you learned how to be 'cool', and apparently eating pizza with a fork and knife was 'in'. She lovingly remembered how Sameer had given up the whole idea and just enjoyed the pizza and their time together while most of them were struggling to even tear a bite.

Sameer offered some more broth to Anaya and asked if Riya needed some.

Chapter 13

As Anaya got busy going through her art supply shopping, Sameer turned her attention towards Riya. It had been driving him nuts, not being the person he is in front of Riya. He believed they had a long history to their name to act like strangers and find it difficult to even talk.

"Look, can we move past this awkwardness? It doesn't suit us. We have known each other since forever."

Riya laughed and nodded in agreement. Hearing her laughter, Sam felt at ease, though still looking at her expectantly. Noticing how intently Sameer was looking at her, she was caught off guard. The laugh had been an instant reaction, a memory of lost familiarity. She remembered laughing a lot whenever she used to be with Sameer.

"You are right. It's just…"

"I know. I know. I understand. I won't ask you anything, I promise." Sam dived in before she could say anything.

"Really?" She raised her eyebrows, mocking him.

"Ok, ok! I may ask you a lot of things, but you can choose not to reply. I swear! But let's not feel this weird strangeness. It drives me insane. Besides, I may not be here for long." He said in one breath.

Hearing him leave churned Riya from within. She had no idea why her body reacted in such a way. He had not been in her life for twelve years, but she was managing fine.

It seemed meeting him here was like a bonus that life threw at her for living her life generously. She had learned how to live without him. Why was she suddenly so sad?

Live without him? Survive is the correct word, Riya.

Is it because subconsciously, her desires had risen, and she wanted him to be close to her again? Or maybe the reaction was a simple disappointment because she had been relishing a familiar face from her life back then. She had nothing left of her from the life she had left behind, and maybe Sameer was the thread that somehow kept her connected to a life she treasured, a life that meant so much to her, a life she had to leave behind, so that she could... survive!

"Riya! Answer me! And moreover, you are looking so beautiful, and I hate not being able to compliment you."

"Sameer! You still are a flirt." Riya laughed at Sameer and shook her head.

Both smiled at the present, how their lives have given them another chance to at least share a meal.

Just then, Riya's phone rang.

As she saw Aarush's name blinking, she excused herself and took the call. Sam observed her smiling and talking in a carefree manner. He could feel insecurity creeping in. All these years, he had always wished for her smiles. But now, when she was right here in front of him, he wanted to be the reason for her smile. He wished he could give her reasons to smile the way she was smiling right now and not be burdened about the deep canyon of twelve years.

He knew he had no right to feel insecure and suddenly felt guilty about it. He realized he should just feel happy about the fact that God has blessed him again with her smile, right in front of him, and not just in the deep crevices of his mind. He shouldn't be thinking about anything else. He should be just glad that she was right here, smiling.

Sameer looked at Riya longingly, thinking that his prayers all these years were being answered after all. *I have given her enough disappointments to be insecure about anything in her life. She is happy, and that's all that matters.*

Sameer's Diary

12th May 2011

Riya!

If a name could cause a whole volcanic eruption inside me, then yours has caused devastation that I am unable to fathom. I miss you deeply.

This is the first time I am writing to you. You always said writing helped with feelings. So I am doing this your way. I thought I would explode from all our suppressed memories. Where are you, Riya? I have exhausted all the places where I could have found you. It seems like the only address you are willing to share with me is my own heart. Maybe you don't want to be found, at least not by me.

I miss you.
I miss your presence.
I miss the way you smile.
I miss being the reason for your smiles.

My daughter reminds me of you. Sometimes I feel she is a younger version of you. She would have loved you. Whenever I look at her, I remember the freshness you filled my life with. Did God bless me with her because I lost you? I don't think God is that gracious, especially towards someone who caused such pain to the one person he always wanted to keep happy.

Riya, I wish to know you are happy, wherever you are.

I don't know if your God will listen to me, but I sincerely pray for your smiles if he does.

Chapter 14

Riya couldn't let go of her feelings. She couldn't believe how her emotions were sailing in a turbulent sea, despite all the years that have passed. She thought she might have forgotten how to sail. But her feelings had the recognition that came with a long-lost habit. Sameer was her guilty pleasure, her habit, her love, her prayer. *Ibaadat!*

She had never been able to bring herself to love someone else. She always looked at men through the lens that had the filter of memories with Sameer. She still couldn't believe she met him in the flesh. All these years, she yearned to hear his voice, but she knew the day she would listen to his voice, she would not be able to breathe. *He did this to her.* He always made her feel like this! She always gasped for breath. He was that monsoon that had given her all the feelings entailed in those love songs, but when it passed, it left her wet and full of the aftermath.

She tried to call Aarush only to find him out of network.

She twisted and turned in her bed, trying to find a position comfortable enough to hold the memories of their love.

Sameer was making the bed and waiting for Anaya to find a book to read. He was in a daze, unable to believe in reality. He couldn't believe that just a few hours back, Riya was sitting with him, sharing a meal and laughing. *Her laugh still lights up everything around.*

Anaya picked 'The Princess Diaries' and brought it to Sameer. He hugged Anaya, and they wrapped themselves in Anaya's blue blanket.

"Papa, Ms. Riya is so beautiful. Do you think she is a princess?"

Sameer was taken aback. Hearing Riya's name from her daughter's lips felt strangely comforting.

"She is a princess. Just like you are!" Sam said sincerely.

Anaya giggled.

"I like how she laughs."

Sameer smiled at her daughter, who had no idea what all her dad loved about Ms. Riya. An entire lifespan wouldn't be enough to tell her how much he loves Riya. But he was surprised at Anaya's feelings and how she noticed such things. Isn't it true that kids are palpable to good and healthy vibes without putting in much effort?

"I want to be like her when I grow up."

"I thought you wanted to be a cricketer."

"That would be my profession, Papa. But I want to be like Ms. Riya. She is so soft. When I hugged her, she hugged me back so warmly."

"Is it?"

"Yes. You should hug her some time and see for yourself."

Sameer smiled at his daughter. He drifted back to the days he had spent in Riya's embrace. He had always loved hugging her, and she had always loved holding his hands. "When I hug you, I am holding my entire universe," he always used to say this to Riya, and she used to blush crimson pink.

There was a peculiar way Riya hugged. *Maybe even hugging is an art.* If you hug too tightly, you make it difficult for the other person to breathe, forcing the hug to end too soon without even feeling the warmth. And hugging too loosely just doesn't make any sense. Why would you even hug if you aren't sincere about it? Riya knew how to hug properly. She was a hugger, if that's even a word. Her hugs were perfect, neither too tight nor too feeble. Whenever she hugged, she made him feel the warmth of their love and promises of togetherness.

There was nothing that her hugs couldn't solve. He found answers to all his uncertainties and fear in her warm hugs.

Chapter 15

For the next few days, Riya busied herself in preparation for her workshop. She had talked to the local authority to organize it in the community center. It was a colossal hall with huge windows that let the sunlight gush in, making it a perfect place for her workshops. She realized that her focus was dwindling and was shifting to Sameer every now and then. She felt like a mother who had to catch her child every time he ran away to play in the dirt, afraid that he may get hurt by the hidden pebbles.

She had decorated the area with colorful ribbons and cut-outs to make it vibrant with energy. She always believed in brightness whenever it came to colors, be it the ambiance, energy, or even the colors themselves. She painted a welcome poster and hung it at the entrance. Inside she put up the easels and canvases. Mrs. Jennie got her freshly made tea and cake and gave some useful tips on managing everything properly.

Finally, on the workshop day, Riya and Mrs. Jennie reached the center well before time. The official time for the workshop was ten o'clock, and participants had started pouring in by nine-thirty.

Riya went inside to make sure everything was in place when she heard a familiar voice coming from outside. She turned around to see Sameer and Anaya.

Anaya beamed at Riya and rushed to hug her.

"Are you also participating, Riya?"

Riya laughed at her innocence.

"Actually, I am the one organizing." She said, pointing at the banner that said her name.

Sameer didn't really pay much attention when Anaya had mentioned the art workshop. Every year Anaya registered in some activity during her spring breaks. He failed to notice who was conducting the workshop. After all, it really didn't matter who was organizing them when it came to art workshops for kids.

After the meal last time, he thought he wouldn't have much chance to see Riya and spend time with her. He had even forgotten to take her contact details. He always lost his sense of being when she was around. But God has been gracious, and here he was, yet again, face to face with Riya.

He was surprised to see Riya's name as the organizer and that the workshop would be conducted by her. *Serendipity*, he thought. But then why was he surprised? This was totally something that Riya would do. She had always loved colors. He remembered how she used to make cards for his birthdays. Even her college room was decorated with simple cut-outs.

Riya was speechless when she turned around to look at Sameer. It had anyway been challenging to keep him off her mind, and here he was. She smiled at him in acknowledgment, well aware of how her heart was playing with her skin.

Sameer was floored with the smile that she radiated. He knew his coming days were going to be absorbed in this workshop. There was no escape. *I will have to move my work around*, he thought to himself as he took out his phone to adjust his work.

As Anaya waved goodbye to Sameer, he said that he would wait here for her rather than go back home. Anaya eyed him suspiciously.

"But you said you have work, and you would come to pick me up later."

Riya smiled to herself as Sameer fumbled to answer. He tried to mend the situation.

"Yes. But I thought I could work here and see you paint."

Anaya shook her head, knowing her dad acts crazy sometimes.

"Okay, but finish your work. Else you will spend the night working, rather than watching movies with me."

Riya instantly knew that Sam moved around his work to be here. There was a jolt of familiarity. She remembered how he always said that he knows his priorities and work always snaked around those. Even when they were together, she could never understand how, despite being busy, he always took out time to be with her or talk to her when they were in different cities. Whenever she asked him about the same, he always tilted his head and smiled at her, "Being with you, talking to you, is like breathing. I do not have to think about it. You do not stop breathing even if you are busy." She smiled at the memory of his voice and the emotions it always stirred within her.

"That's one smart daughter you have." Riya looked inquiringly at Sam.

"Like father, like daughter." Sam quipped and flashed his ever-charming smile, making Riya lose her footing.

Mrs. Jennie walked towards Riya and shook her shoulder.

"Shouldn't you start?"

Embarrassed, Riya introduced them to each other and started walking towards the paints when Mrs. Jennie called out to her.

"By the way, that brat called to wish you luck."

"Aarush? He called you?"

Suddenly Sameer's ears shot up at the name.

"You know him better than that!" Mrs. Jennie rolled her eyes. "You left your phone on the porch on the breakfast table. Luckily, I heard it ringing and answered. At least he remembers things related to you."

"I doubt it. I am sure he wanted to just remind me of the embarrassing moment from that one workshop. Jerk!"

Chapter 16

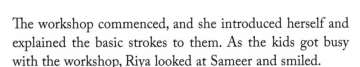

The workshop commenced, and she introduced herself and explained the basic strokes to them. As the kids got busy with the workshop, Riya looked at Sameer and smiled.

"Are you really working?" She went to Sameer and asked, looking at the blank screen on his laptop.

"What? Of course!"

"Really!" Riya rolled her eyes, knowing very well that Sameer was distracted and far from working.

"Well, nothing is as precious as watching people engrossed in art." He grinned and continued, "Especially those whom I love."

Riya shook her head, knowing very well that he was flirting again. She pointed towards his laptop, signaling him to work. Sameer raised his hands in surrender and got back to his work with a huge grin.

For the next hour, Riya was busy working with the kids, showing them how to blend the colors, holding their hands, and teaching them the amount of pressure required. Sameer lifted his eyes from the laptop and found Riya holding a girl's hand and working slowly and tenderly.

"I wish it was my hand that she was holding. Look at her smile!" Mrs. Jennie heard his comment and coughed next to him. He straightened, unaware of the fact that she was close by.

"Looking at her from here won't help. It will just make you lose your precious breaths by sighing continuously."

"What? No, No. Mrs. Jennie. I was not… I was looking at Anaya." He fumbled as he tried to find Anaya.

Mrs. Jennie scoffed and held his chin, and shifted it to the right. "Then this is where you look."

Sam blushed. "Am I that obvious?"

"To my old eyes, you are a bag of feelings just waiting to burst open and spill the contents on her."

Sameer was at a loss of words. He didn't know what to say to defend himself.

Am I again hoping for love? I shouldn't make her go through it when I have so much baggage. I cannot be so selfish.

"It is okay to be selfish sometimes when you are sure about the fact that both the people want the same things. But make sure you do want the same things!"

Sam looked at Mrs. Jennie wide-eyed and leaned a little away from her.

"Are you a psychic or something?"

Mrs. Jennie smiled at him and patted his head, and moved towards the painting area.

Chapter 17

Sameer was restless the whole night after returning from the workshop. He could not focus anywhere. Mrs. Jennie's words were spinning in his head. It was like being lost amidst the whirlpool of thoughts. He wasn't sure if it was her words or his feelings that were making him dizzy.

He had no idea how Riya felt about him after all these years, especially after what happened between them. He couldn't stop wondering if he still affected her in some way. Before knowing anything about her feelings, he knew he couldn't take a plunge. He wasn't even sure if they should even take the plunge as he did not want to make Riya suffer any more than she already has because of him. His thoughts kept gushing and eroding the memories that had settled on the surface over the years.

What do we have to lose? Maybe this is a second chance that God has blessed us with. If not now, then it's never gonna happen ever again.

Despite such overwhelmingly positive thoughts, there was something that held him back. He could not stop thinking how selfish he was by expecting Riya to still want to be with him, especially with all the baggage that came with him.

But Riya always said that you should be selfish in love. Didn't we lose each other once because we weren't selfish enough?

Just while he was trying to manage these tumbling thoughts, a voice in his head yelled at him.

You! You weren't selfish enough!

He didn't know what Riya felt about them. All he knew was that Riya was, and still is, the person who makes his heart flutter and has the power to put him at ease. She was that irony in his life that could make his heart beat at an insane rate and at the same time could make him feel at peace.

He remembered their conversation from just before his wedding.

"I will be there for your wedding."

"Riya, are you sure?"

"Of course. I am being selfish, Sameer. I love to see you happy. It gives me happiness. I will be there for my peace." Riya had said, gathering all the courage she thought she could summon.

He had promised Riya to be happy in his marriage, the only thing that Riya ever asked of him with full right.

He never denied the fact that there were times when he lay awake at night, thinking about her smile. He genuinely tried to be happy. But sooner than later, he realized that there is a difference between being happy and seeking happiness. Half his efforts were invested in seeking moments of joy throughout his marriage rather than just being happy.

It was Riya's smile that had kept him sane during the darkest hours of his life. The knowledge that his happiness would matter to Riya, wherever she was, was enough for him to carry forward with his life.

Chapter 18

It was the second day of the workshop. Not finding Sameer anywhere around disappointed Riya a little. She didn't expect Sameer to be there for the workshop's entire duration, but she secretly hoped that he would be there. She knew she should not be hoping like that since such kinds of expectations, more often than not, end up disappointing you.

She focused on her workshop and lost track of time. After a while, she moved around the little artists, looking at their work and appreciating them in every possible way. She knew it was necessary to keep them motivated and happy.

"Hi. How is it going?" Riya was taken aback by a familiar voice. Just when she had stopped looking for Sameer, he appeared, *like always*.

"Hey." She said, trying to hide the huge smile that was trying to escape her lips. "As good as it can get. No work today like last time?" Riya said, noticing his casual look. She didn't want to accept that his casual attitude was making her toes curl and insides flip with desire.

"Hey. What is it with you and my work?"

"I am worried you will be dependent on me for food and a place soon." Riya teased him. Contrary to the reaction Riya expected, Sameer smiled and ignored whatever Riya said, knowing how much he would want both of them to be dependent on each other, not just for food and a place but for everything else as well.

Relationships are strange. When you are in love, you want to be dependent on each other, as if it is one of the ways you feel closer. But if the relationship is not based on love, this dependency burdens the bond and sooner or later ruins it.

"So, when did you start taking workshops?" Sameer shifted the conversation to a lesser controversial subject.

"It has been some time. A few years back, I had put up my work in one of the exhibitions organized by Mrs. Jennie, when one of the school teachers came and gave me the idea for a workshop during these vacations."

"She didn't offer you to teach in school?"

"Actually, that's what she asked me to do initially. But I was not really sure of such a commitment. Moreover..."

"Moreover, if you taught in a school, you would have to go by the syllabus and won't be able to explore, which kills the essence of creativity." Sameer completed the sentence for her and smiled.

Riya looked at him and smiled at the familiarity of words. It was rare to meet people who had similar mindsets and perspectives towards life. Sameer and Riya complimented each other on how they lived their lives, making them an entity in themselves.

Years back, when they were hunting for jobs, Sameer had come across a teaching position. But he had declined the offer saying that if you joined schools or colleges with a set curriculum, it restricts your imagination from exploring what is beyond the black and white of the curriculum.

It had been long since she was with someone who knew her heart. Sometimes familiarity aches in the right places and makes you aware of everything you have been missing.

"It's true," Sam stated, opening his laptop.

"What?"

"People don't really change much over time. Their core values almost remain the same. Probably that's why it's easy to start again where you left years back."

Riya looked at Sam as her heart skipped a beat. He held her gaze with gentleness. If eyes could speak, this would have been the most intense discussion of should-not, could-not, must-not, ifs and buts, should-be, could-be, must-be.

It had hardly been a few days since Sameer breezed in her life, and it already felt like he had never left. The way they felt for each other even after twelve years was enough proof to show that the heart knows what it wants. It can pick up from where it left. *If only we, as humans, realize it sooner.*

"Things are so different now," Riya said, looking at the kids engrossed in their work.

"Life is always in a state of perpetual motion. How else would you know that time has passed? But what makes you say so?" Sameer wasn't sure what Riya meant. Was she talking about things between them or something else?

"Look at all these kids, so serious about art. When we were their age, we were either busy sleeping or running around with our neighborhood friends, playing gully cricket. Nobody bothered exploring the hidden talents, let alone improving them. We used to just enjoy being kids without homework."

"Yeah. That's true. When I look at Anaya and all the different camps and workshops she wants to attend, it drives me crazy. I didn't even know such things existed when I was her age. Our life was sorted."

"I think the difference also lies in the education system. Here, kids explore diverse things along with the regular subjects. Back in India, it's different. You have to focus solely on a few subjects."

"Yeah, you could say so." Sameer was also deep in thought.

"How did Anaya manage to switch to the US education system?" Riya asked after thinking for a while.

Sameer looked at Riya with a sad smile. "We came here when she was 1. So, she has always been studying here only."

Riya was taken aback. Sameer had been here in The States for so many years. He hated any place that did not have bidets in restrooms. He loved being in India with all the chaos that came with the Indian culture, and the ever-eavesdropping Indian society.

She couldn't even start to imagine how Sameer must have managed to raise Anaya. *Where was his wife? Did she also move with them?* She had not seen her with them any of these days. She wished she could ask all these questions, more out of concern than curiosity.

"Was it hard?" Riya asked slowly. Sameer looked at Riya, trying to understand what she wanted to know. Riya continued, "I mean sending Anaya to school, raising her, taking her to such workshops, you know. Was it… is it hard being a father?"

The look in Sameer's eyes left Riya speechless. For a second, she could not recognize the flamboyant and carefree Sameer that she had known. All she could see in those eyes were long, restless nights, hard decisions that had to be taken, and lots of guilt. Yes, she saw it there; guilt and regret.

"It is difficult in the initial years because you don't know what is expected of you. You have no idea how to be responsible for a small child who depends entirely on you, your decisions, and your perspectives of reality. But you get used to it, and eventually, it feels like a new normal."

"And what about Anaya?"

"I have been very fortunate, Riya, when it comes to Anaya. She is a lifesaver. I know it should be the opposite, but I feel proud to accept that she is the one who has helped me adapt and enjoy my new normal. Do you remember, I always used to tell you that I would spoil my kids?" He smiled at the memory and continued, "Anaya spoils me. She is way too mature for her age. She has the maturity of a teenager but without the teenage tantrums. Sometimes I wonder where she learned all that wisdom she spills on me every now and then. She is my biggest strength and my biggest weakness, you know!" He looked longingly at Anaya, "I want to be an amazing dad to her. I know it is quite selfish, but I want her to love me deeply. I don't know what I would have done or who I would have been without her in my life. She is the yin to my yang."

Deep within, an instinct made her realize that Sameer raised her alone. *Something happened to his marriage, and quite early in the days.*

Hearing such words from Sameer made her realize how life demands you to change with time. The carefree Sameer she had known was now a dad who wanted to be responsible for her daughter. The guy who flirted around vivaciously wants his daughter to love him deeply. She was somehow proud of how Sameer had grown as a person.

She realized that this is how you charge ahead in life. Sameer accepted his reality and embraced it with his innate *Sameerness.* He might have temporarily questioned his choices and his fate, but he accepted what life threw at him with open arms. He was someone who always knew how to let life guide you, unlike herself. She had tried to resist the change and had suffered. She struggled through every twist and turn just because she was naive enough not to understand that life itself has its own whims and fancies, to pay heed to yours too.

Chapter 19

Riya was sitting on their common porch when Mrs. Jennie came and handed her a cup of herbal mint tea. She was satisfied with the workshop's result, but her mind kept drifting back to Sameer and their conversation.

"How was today's workshop, darling? Mrs. Jennie asked, tucking Riya's hair away from her face.

"It was great, Mrs. Jennie. There is so much talent in such young kids. And they work so hard."

"Yes. It's good they are spending more time in creating art than on the screens." Mrs. Jennie rolled her eyes. She looked at Riya, who was still looking far away, lost in her own world. "Was Sameer there today as well?"

Riya nodded.

"And?"

"He has grown so much, Mrs. Jennie. I really admire him for the person he has become. I feel he is a great father."

"Are you doing okay?"

Riya looked at Mrs. Jennie. She knew she was talking about Sameer. She let out a sigh.

"Frankly speaking, Mrs. Jennie, I don't know. We are not acting like strangers, at least, which is a big relief. Sometimes I want to give myself a second chance, but then I feel if it is even worth the effort."

"Really? Of all the things, you doubt if it is *worth the effort?*"

Riya was fazed by Mrs. Jennie's words.

"How do you see through me so well?" Riya shook her head, knowing that Mrs. Jennie was right, "Actually, deep within, I know he is worth all the effort, not just today but in all the lifetimes. And frankly, that is what scares me. He affects me so much even now, Mrs. Jennie. When he talks like a mature father, he makes me realize how well he has adapted to being an adult. And I am so proud of him. When he smiles or flirts, he brings back college memories and makes me feel like the person I was twelve years ago. I feel innocent and pure again. But I don't know if I even want to feel like that."

"Don't be so hard on yourself and stop introspecting too much. What have I always told you? It always makes things worse. You take life too seriously, my love."

"Mrs. Jennie."

"I don't know what you two shared in the past or have endured all these years. All I know is, sometimes destiny and coincidences play along together, just to confuse us. If your heart wants to go for it, even for a second, go for it. Nothing could feel worse than those few months after he got married. Isn't it?"

Riya nodded, understanding what Mrs. Jennie was trying to say. Mrs. Jennie looked at the forlorn figure in front of her, held her chin, and made Riya face her. "And nothing feels worse than missed chances, especially second ones."

"So, you mean we should give it a try?" Riya said cautiously, with hope shining in her eyes. It is strange how our eyes directly convey what our heart really wants when our faces and mind are still trying to argue about the right thing to do.

"How are you so sure that he also wants to be with you?" Mrs. Jennie pointed out, smiling at Riya's expressions.

"Oh!" Riya suddenly felt disheartened, as if she was as close as possible to have that last piece of chocolate, and it fell. She had assumed that Sameer was also feeling what she had been feeling all these days.

"See, now you are sure of at least your feelings." Mrs. Jennie smiled warmly at Riya and patted her head.

Riya's Diary

17th January 2011

Sameer,

It has been four years and seven months since I heard your voice. Telling you, "I miss you" would be an understatement. I don't know how to explain it to you, but sometimes I feel I miss the sensations your voice created more than I miss you. I miss the feeling of my name when it escaped from your lips. Your voice was like a security blanket for me, a blanket that I lost. I wish I could have kept at least a few scraps of it. But I never knew that a day would come when it won't be there to lull me to sleep.

Life hasn't been merciful since you left, but the only thing that keeps me going is your happiness. I hope you are doing great and being happy. Because if not, we are paying a heavy price for nothing.

Sometimes I wish I could forget you, but then I am not willing to let go of the feeling of being in love with you. It was one of the best feelings my soul ever experienced. I knew it would be a disaster to even want to forget you, so I never even tried doing that. I thought I would remember you as my best-kept memory, without all the melodrama that comes with missing someone. But remembering you makes me feel every inch of my soul and how agonizing it is since you aren't here. I wish I could fill the vacuum in every cell of my body that your absence has created.

None of the memories make sense anymore.

Those were treasured memories because we both were there in it. With you gone, now they all seem like a paracosm? How do I explain? It's like I am the only person in those memories now, and everything that we once shared seems singular.

I miss you so much that it aches!

Chapter 20

Both Riya & Sameer started eagerly waiting for 9:30 am, looking forward to spending those stolen moments from the workshop with each other.

"Looks like you are somewhere else." Riya said, sipping the tea Mrs. Jennie brought with her today.

"Yes. I am inside an R&D lab's data storage bank." Sameer replied without moving his eyes from the laptop screen.

"What? Isn't that illegal?"

"It is. For you!" Sameer turned to Riya with a smug.

"You know your arrogance hasn't changed at all!" She shook her head and offered him a cup.

"Thanks. I am freelancing for a government project on data breach in several R&D departments." Looking at how lost Riya looked, he explained, "Basically, I am authorized by the security department."

"Wow! That's impressive!"

"What do you think I keep doing on my laptop then?" Sameer asked, amused with Riya's expressions.

"Playing games?" Riya said skeptically, knowing very well that he wasn't a gaming person.

"What? Really! You underestimate me so much." Sam commented in an overly dramatic manner.

"What? That's nonsense. I always believed in you."

Sameer looked at Riya intently before replying, "Actually, yes! You have always believed in me more than I believed in myself." Sam said sincerely and got back to his work.

Riya was perplexed at the sudden change in the tone of the conversation. This is what dislodged her from reality. First, his presence in flesh and bones, then, his statements, and worst of all, his statements, and the worst of all, his eyes!

She realized that amidst this bickering and teasing each other, they actually found their comfort and forgot that they are past twelve years to those days when they found solace in each other. Their unconscious mind brought them back to the same feelings they both so desperately wanted to express but were being careful not to.

She noticed Sameer concentrating and working hard and remembered how diligently he used to prepare for his Master's entrance exams. She remembered how he waited for her calls early in the morning to wish him luck for his exams and how she waited for his exams to finish every day so that she could know how it went. She remembered the morning he excitedly called her after getting through one of the best courses in IT security. She remembered how she savored the sound of his voice when he used to blabber about the college frustrations, how she realized that she had fallen irrevocably in love with her oldest friend.

Looking at him, Riya realized he still was the same person who was her first kiss, her first love, and whose happiness meant the world to her.

It's not every day that people love the way they had loved each other. Even now, she always felt proud of being able to love someone with such sincerity.

Chapter 21

It was the last day of the workshop, and there was always fun and frolic on the last day of her workshops. Riya had invited the family members of the participants too. After all, it is always a pleasure to see your kids reach a level you never anticipated.

Sam was standing next to Mrs. Jennie's counter of cakes, serving cakes, all the while keeping her eyes on Riya. He had been observing Riya the whole evening. She was smoothly gliding amongst the parents, taking in the compliments with utmost modesty. Her smile was lightening the entire plaza. She looked ethereal to Sam in her white dress with pink stars.

Mrs. Jennie had been observing Sam, and she noticed that he rarely took his eyes off Riya. He was marveling at how she was the star of the evening.

He saw Riya picking up her phone and talking animatedly to whoever was on the other side of the phone. Sam observed her laughing, frowning, smiling, blushing, and almost all the expressions any human is capable of.

"Isn't she wonderful?" Mrs. Jennie teased Sam.

"Yes, she is." Sam sighed without taking his eyes off Riya.

"She is the happiest during these workshops."

"I can spend my entire life looking at her smile."

Mrs. Jennie laughed. Sam suddenly realized what happened. Before he could say anything, he saw Riya disconnecting the phone and approaching them. She was giddy with happiness at the success of this workshop.

"Aarush says *hola* from Cuba." She said to Mrs. Jennie, mimicking Aarush. "He wanted to know if I broke a leg in this workshop too. I told you that was the only reason he was trying to call the first day too." Riya said, rolling her eyes.

"She tumbled on the stage 4 years back and sprained her leg while explaining a brushstroke. And since then, we vowed never to have a stage ever again." Mrs. Jennie explained to Sam, who was fidgeting uncomfortably. He was feeling like an outsider in this conversation. It seemed to him that he was twelve years behind, and there was a lot of catching up to do. The more he tried to figure out who Aarush is to Riya, the more he felt confused. "He will never let you forget that." Mrs. Jennie looked at Riya and laughed.

"He was born to embarrass me!" Riya shook her head and was about to leave when Anaya came jumping towards them. She asked Sam to dance with Riya, who hesitated a bit.

"Come on. It's such a lively evening. I wish I had a partner to dance with." Mrs. Jennie made a face.

"Don't worry, Mrs. Jennie." Sam bowed and offered his hand to Mrs. Jennie. "May I have the pleasure of dancing with you?" Anaya laughed at her dad as Mrs. Jennie shook her head.

"You are too old school for me, darling. Perhaps Riya suits you more." She winked at Sam, and Sam returned a huge grin.

Sam asked Riya, and she reluctantly placed her hand in his. He took control of the dance right from the first step.

After a few seconds on the dance floor, Sam bent forward towards her ears and whispered. "Can you look at me and dance?"

Riya flushed red and looked down. "Come on. I know you are trying too hard to control yourself as I look so hot in this suit. But at least look at me!"

Riya punched him with her elbow. "Hey! Come on!"

Riya finally looked at him, and he started moving again. He felt his heart dancing to a completely different tune. He could feel Riya's heart beating next to his. He loved how she always fits in his arms so perfectly. As for Riya, she knew this was a completely different kind of dancing. It was pure!

They could feel how their bodies responded to each other.

He was lost in her aura when he was interrupted on his journey to etherealness.

"You are a jerk, you know," Riya said after a while.

"What did I do?" Sam was taken aback. He knew she was teasing him.

"I know where your eyes have been wandering for the whole evening today." She blushed as she said this.

"Oh! So, someone knew that she was being watched!" Sam grinned.

"You will never change." She smiled affectionately at him.

"Do you want me to?" Sam stopped dancing and looked at her.

Riya was at a loss for words as she sensed the intensity in his eyes. *She knew these eyes.* She knew what this look meant. She knew that Sameer meant every word he said just now. And if she asked him to change, he would. He would change anything for her. And this knowledge scared her.

The silence between them was broken by a commotion at the end of the plaza. A girl slipped a glass and broke it. Riya came to her senses and rushed to the girl. Everything settled after a while, and everyone started leaving.

"Riya! Thank you for such an amazing workshop." Anaya hugged her.

Riya kissed her forehead.

"Papa, can we invite her over for dinner?" Anaya asked, holding Sameer's hand.

"Of course, if Ms. Riya doesn't have any other commitments."

Damn this guy. He has started teasing her again, Riya thought to herself.

Sam helped her pack everything and loaded it in Mrs. Jennie's car. Before Sam got in his car, Mrs. Jennie held his elbow and looked him in his eyes.

"It's rare for a man to be so engrossed by the happiness that he feels when he sees the person he loves flaring effortlessly. A man like this deserves all the second chances in life."

Sam looked at her and couldn't believe what she just said. Mrs. Jennie smiled and kissed him on his cheeks, and walked away towards her car.

Chapter 22

Sam drove towards his home with Anaya in the passenger seat and Riya behind. He noticed that she had rolled the windows down. He knew she was either lost in her thoughts or may just be feeling the breeze with an empty mind.

Sam adjusted his rear mirror and gazed at Riya. The wind was blowing hair on her face. He felt a sudden bolt of jealousy for being unable to touch her hair and play with it.

The evening had been good to them. He was especially happy for Riya, who effortlessly pulled off such a massive workshop. He was marveling at her skills and how she bloomed amidst all the colors. He realized what Mrs. Jennie observed. He was really proud of Riya and her work. He was feeling immense bliss seeing Riya bask in all the glory.

His thoughts shifted gears and slid smoothly towards their dance and the small yet deep conversation they had. It was strange how even a few words between them made a whole lot of sense than an hour-long conversation with someone else. He knew what she felt at that moment from the way she looked at him.

You might have scared her. Idiot!

Oh, but how much I want to be there for her!

Anaya yelled as Sam was about to miss the parkway. He pulled the brakes, and the car came to a sudden halt.

"Sorry," Sam said to no one in particular.

Sam opened the door of his home, and Anaya rushed in with her painting. He stood by the door, holding it open for Riya as she walked in, brushing against his chest; Sam's eyes never left her.

She looked around and took in the ambiance. Sam walked past her and put the keys on a tray painted "S & A" in a haggard manner. He gestured towards the other door as Riya asked for the washroom.

Riya walked cautiously towards the washroom, aware of her surroundings. She closed the door behind her and rested her head against the door, and exhaled. She had been holding her breath for a long time now. How can he affect her so much? *It is just a dinner, not a date. Yes, but at his house, not a restaurant.* She knew his eyes were on her for the entire drive from the plaza to home. She couldn't stop thinking about what Sam had asked her while dancing. She knew he was being immensely sincere when he asked if she would like him to change. She remembered Mrs. Jennie's advice.

I think we both are on the same page.

She dried her hands and came out to find Sam holding a chef knife and wearing a funny-looking apron.

"So, what do you think?" Sam gestured towards himself, wearing the apron.

"Looks like you custom-made the apron to fit your size."

"Aah. Someone is checking out my body. Anaya, I told you your dad is a charmer!" Sam grinned. Anaya giggled as Riya hit him on his shoulder and moved to the other side to wash the veggies.

"Hey, don't cut them julienne." Sameer stopped Riya suddenly while she was cutting veggies for dinner. Looking at the questioning face, he explained, "Anaya doesn't like veggies sticking around the insides of her cheeks."

"It feels as if some worms are poking me." Anaya chimed in. Riya smiled at her and chopped the veggies some more, and showed it to Sameer. He gave her a thumbs up and went back to his marinating.

They got absorbed in cooking with expert comments coming from Anaya every now and then.

"Riya, how long have you been friends with Papa?" Anaya asked, looking at Riya with big brown eyes. Riya stopped midway and looked at Sameer, who answered it for her.

"More than you have known that blue blanket of yours."

Anaya blushed. "Oh, more than eleven years! Did you also not let anybody else touch each other like I don't let anyone touch my blanket?"

Sameer was overcome with emotions for his daughter. He walked towards her and gave her a kiss as she bombarded them with questions from their college life and little knick-knacks. Sameer and Riya were teleported to their college life as they related funny incidents from that time to Anaya.

Simultaneously, they set the table and sat down to eat. The room was filled with laughter and an aroma of bliss.

"Looks like you have learned how to cook!" Riya commented as she enjoyed the meal.

Sam raised his wine glass in acknowledgment.

"Papa is a great cook. Even my friends love it when I bring them food after my breaks."

"Really? I am impressed."

"Papa is very impressive. That's why there are so many girls in his office who like him."

Riya let out a chuckle. "Oh really! Aren't you too small to know about them, little girl?"

"I am his best friend. Isn't it, papa?" Anaya looked towards Sameer with a proud expression in her eyes.

"Of course, my love. You are my best friend." Sameer held her little hands and kissed them. Riya looked at them with warm adoration.

"Who is your best friend, Riya?" Anaya turned towards Riya as she took a bite of her toast.

She could sense Sameer's eyes on her. Riya thought for a while before answering. "Can you be my best friend?"

"Really? It would be fun. You can also be papa's best friend."

"Anaya!"

"Come on, papa. You have been old friends with Riya. I think she will be an excellent friend now also."

"But he already has a best friend. You are his best friend." Riya ruffled her hair.

"Sometimes he needs grown-up friends when he is alone, and I am at school. And those friends in the office, who like papa, are not very good."

Riya looked at Sameer, whose breathing had slowed to a murmur.

"So, does your papa also like any of those girls?"

Anaya turned to Riya and said, "He doesn't like anyone. I also don't like them. They wear so much lipstick."

"Your papa does not like lipstick?"

"Don't you know? He hates it." Anaya giggled.

"Then what does he like? Let's find someone without lipstick for him and who you also like."

"I like you. You are perfect!"

Sameer coughed. Riya didn't realize when the conversation took a turn towards this. She stole a glance at Sameer, who was trying to pick a noodle for the last 5 minutes.

"Anaya, don't eat while you talk." Sameer quipped suddenly.

Riya and Anaya turned to Sameer and laughed at how he mistakenly twisted the words. Anaya got busy eating the noodles, and for a while, the conversation died down.

"So, you sprained your leg?"

"What? Oh ya. Nothing serious. But it was embarrassing. That workshop was for college students, and I was so engrossed that I missed the edge and fell." She laughed at herself.

"Did it not hurt?" Sam asked in a tone that was as serious as a doctor telling you bad news. The ambiguity of the question left Riya at a loss for an answer. She wasn't sure if Sameer wanted to know about her leg or something else totally.

She occupied herself with her food and let the question linger. They finished their meal and cleaned up the kitchen. Anaya went to her study room and settled herself. Sam weighed his options of asking about Aarush. Before he could think it through and filter through the layers of adulting, he spilled it out.

"So, who is Aarush?" He asked cautiously, knowing that her answer may change his life yet again.

"Papa, can we please sleep?" Before Riya could answer, Anaya yelled from the study room. He got up and carried her upstairs to her room.

Riya refilled her wine and walked around the house, taking in the knick-knacks that resembled Sameer's habits. She was looking at the backyard garden when he came.

"She slept?" Riya asked, sipping her wine.

Sam nodded.

"It's beautiful here. You have maintained this so well." She said, admiring the garden.

"I enjoy working with the mud. And it's a totally different feeling when all the flowers bloom." Sam said happily with a shine in his eyes.

"Yeah, I can see that. You have almost all the colors here."

"Someone I knew loved colors," Sam said, turning towards her.

They sat on the steps with their feet in the wet mud. It had rained in the afternoon, so the weather was pleasant and less humid.

Riya wrapped her scarf more tightly. Sam realized she was feeling cold. He got up and brought a throw from inside. He wrapped it around Riya and him. They talked about things in general and laughed over silly things. They would look like a very content couple enjoying wine under a starry night to anyone looking at them. The comfort they felt was palpable. Neither of them was making an effort. It was as smooth as fluid as if that's how it was supposed to be.

They were silent for a while when Riya finally asked Sam about his life.

"So, if you don't mind me asking. What happened?"

Sameer took a moment before answering, weighing the amount of information that he wanted to convey. He sighed.

"You were there when I got married." Sam said this quickly as if to get over it without letting her dwell on that day. "But then it didn't work out. So, we mutually agreed to separate."

"You are telling it so casually as if it is someone else's story."

"It didn't feel like mine," Sam said with a hint of sadness in his voice.

"And Anaya?"

"Same old story. We thought having a kid would bring us closer."

Riya looked at him with questioning eyes.

"Yeah, I know. It sounds like a cliche and so unlike me. And educated people like us should know better than that. But when your marriage isn't working, you try every other thing to make sure it does. Your own reasoning stops, and you listen to what everyone around has to say and follow it."

"So how does it work with Anaya now?"

"We have joint custody. We keep meeting during her breaks from boarding school. She remarried, so there aren't many complications. So... yeah, it's all cool. I guess." As Riya sat there absorbing these new pieces of Sameer's life, he looked at Riya and said, "Should I tell you a secret?"

"Absolutely."

"Anaya loves being with me. She likes me more than her mom."

"Oh my God!" She said, rolling her eyes, "And the self-obsessed heart of yours would revel in this feeling. Isn't it?" Riya teased Sameer.

"Of course!" Sameer smiled. "So ya, that's how it was... it is. How did you know?"

"Know what?"

"About my unsuccessful attempt at marriage."

"I don't know, really. Instinct maybe! I know you enough to understand that something went wrong. You didn't talk about her all these days. And I know how much you love to talk about the people you love. Moreover, she wasn't there during the entire workshop. So, I assumed that things might not have been good."

"Looks like you have again been overthinking." Sameer smiled at Riya as he sipped his wine.

"Or maybe I never stopped thinking," Riya whispered to no one in particular, but loud enough for Sameer to hear. She controlled her emotions and turned to him, strong enough to ask about his life. "Was it hard? Going through it all?"

"Of course, it was hard, Riya. You know it better than anyone else how much I want my family to be happy, and I wanted my marriage to work. God knows how much I wanted it to succeed. We both put in efforts, but eventually, we realized we were struggling to even be someone else to please each other. It was like most of our efforts went into trying to keep it all together rather than being with each other. I feel guilty when I say this, but the best time of my day was when I used to come back home, and she was fast asleep, and I could have Anaya all to myself."

Riya moved her hand over his and traced his palms with her fingers.

"And that's it. She got an opportunity here, so she moved here earlier with Anaya. I tried to survive Ahmedabad, but it was full of memories and regrets." He looked solemnly at Riya as if trying to express his regret at losing memories with her as well. "And frankly, I missed Anaya so badly that it started to ache. After a few months, I moved here as well, and here we are."

"I am sorry. I wish I knew." Riya said slowly, feeling crippled by the sadness he might have felt all those years back.

"You had disappeared as if punishing me for my decisions," Sameer said with a hint of sorrow.

"I am sorry." Riya was at a loss for words.

"Don't be. I am the one who is sorry for making you want to disappear."

The silence hung around them while they sipped their wine.

"What about you? Who is Aarush?" Sameer suddenly changed the tone of his voice.

Riya smiled. She didn't even realize that Aarush's presence might be hanging like a wall in front of Sameer.

"He is my best friend. We have known each other for quite some years now."

"Just best friends?"

"Sameer!"

Sameer felt at peace. He exhaled as if he was holding his breath since Aarush had kept his hand around Riya's shoulders when they had met momentarily at Starbucks.

"And marriage?"

Riya shrugged and let the question hang. She was taking some time for herself to commit to what she was about to say.

"Never felt right with **anyone else**." She said, looking at him, putting extra stress on the last two words.

Chapter 23

Sometimes it's better to react when you have less information. Because more often than not, the heaviness of knowledge weighs down on your heart. Sameer was at a loss of words. They sat there silently as it started raining. The fragrance of wet earth rekindled their emotions, so did the wine.

"So, what do you say? Should we complete that dance we left at the plaza?" Sameer said, drunk on the wine, thereby with lowered inhibitions. He pulled Riya towards him, and she fell in his arms. The inhibitions that control the emotions during the day had left them bare. More than the steps, Sameer could feel electricity dancing between them. The wine did its work, lowering their guard down, and they were doing theirs by giving way to their emotions.

Sameer pulled Riya closer from her waist. He moved his other free hand over her arm. Riya's heart was thumping against her chest. She knew this wasn't right, but she was fine being wrong. They had anyway lost each other by wanting to be correct. Sameer was looking in her eyes with passion and could feel her breath. He would have wanted to take her right there, right then, and both of them knew nothing else would have mattered.

It is a pity when such intense desire lays dormant for quite a long time.

He moved his thumb over her cheeks and traced those laughter lines down to the corner of her lips. He could feel

89

Riya clutching his shirt. He had missed this sensation of her fingers digging deep in his skin through his shirt. He moved his hand in her hair and opened her bun.

Riya was dizzy with the influx of all these emotional chemicals. She wasn't sure if it was the wine or him that had activated those triggers. She looked into his eyes, the ones that had held her most precious memories; the eyes that made her feel like the most beautiful girl in the world.

He moved his fingers over her lower back where he had held her and pressed her towards him. He was suddenly possessive about her and didn't want the space between them to claim even an inch of her body.

Their legs' movement was as incidental as the remnants of chocolate left in the wrapper.

Sameer felt the heat. He knew another moment of closeness, and years of longing could have swept them into something they both were not sure of. He took a step back, breaking the moment, and looked down. Riya suddenly realized what could have happened. She was disappointed. She wanted to let go of herself!

"It's quite late. Let me walk you back to your apartment." He said cautiously, not entirely wanting to believe the amount of strength he had to gather to take a step back.

"Oh no. Anaya may wake up. She will worry then. I'll manage." She hurried towards the door, embarrassed at what she was thinking. *Actually, not thinking.*

"Riya." Sam pulled her from her elbow as she stumbled over his chest. He looked deep into her eyes. He had so much to say to her, but he let it all hang between them. "I can't let you go alone. You are drunk already." She was looking at him innocently. He had always found this viridity endearing.

He wanted to take her to his room and caress those quivering lips and trace every single goosebump that was there on her skin.

"Ummm... do you... maybe... if it's ok, want to stay here for the night?"

"I don't know if it's..."

They could feel the uncertainty of the moment. It was strange how after the most intimate moments, awkwardness creeps in.

"There is a spare room upstairs."

"Sameer. I don't know." Sam knew she would be unsure of everything right now. He had to be strong for her. He knew he didn't want to take a step under the effect of alcohol and taint the purity of their relation.

"Riya. It's after midnight. You cannot walk back. You cannot drive since you drank, and I cannot take any chances with uber at this hour. Don't worry. You can leave first thing in the morning. Okay?"

She loved the authority in his voice whenever he cared for her. Riya nodded, and Sameer headed upstairs to get her the covers.

What am I doing? I should just leave. He doesn't want to be with me. He just took a step back. You are a fool!

Maybe he was just trying to do the right thing.

Riya turned to leave when Sam came and gave her the covers. Seeing that she was about to leave, he took a step towards her.

"Riya."

She looked at him as if asking to shed all his inhibitions and let the emotions take charge.

He took a step forward, held her face, and kissed her forehead.

"I am right here."

He tugged her hair behind her ears, smiled warmly at her, and headed upstairs to his room.

Sameer's Diary

18th September 2017

I hope you are doing well, Riya. I hope you have become a sensational artist by now. I miss your charming smile.

Yesterday I was lazily lying on my chair, overlooking the beach, while Anaya played with her kitchen set. I started dreaming about you. It is such a fantastic feeling when your mind unconsciously wanders to someone, especially someone who occupies your soul.

I imagined cooking breakfast together, with your hair tied in a bun, as if you have been busy preparing the meal, even though Anaya and I have been great helping hands. Okay! Okay! You can exclude me. I would be too busy to admire how adept you are at frying eggs. I could hear the laughter and bliss that resonated in our kitchen. I dreamt of having a hearty meal together and going out for a walk because I know how much you love to walk around. I hope someday we can sit together at a curbside cafe, observe people and have fun.

Isn't it strange how one random thought can trigger your dearest dreams? Especially the ones that you had hidden deep in the abyss of your heart! I miss having a life with you, Riya.

Lately, I have come to realize that even the mundanity of domestic life would have been fun, sharing it with you. I know I do not deserve these moments with you. Sorry for thinking this, especially after what I did to us. But like I told you, it all just sort of started jumping around without any conscious effort.

Knowing you has made me a better person, Riya. I hope I am no more a thorn in your life. I hope you remember me, if you do at all, with fondness.

You were and are a blessing to me and my heart.

I am proud of being loved by you, Riya.

Chapter 24

Sameer knew he had disappointed Riya tonight. He could tell by looking at her eyes. But alcohol often lowers a person's inhibitions, and he had to be sure what Riya wanted, with all her senses intact, before he could take any step towards her.

The knowledge that Riya was right there in the next room made him vulnerable. He couldn't sleep even for a second. The moment he closed his eyes, the memories from twelve years ago came flashing. Those late-night calls to her when she would just listen to what he had to say, the drunken calls, the success story calls, the life-sucks calls. They had been through so much together. He could never forget that it was Riya who taught him the meaning of friendship and love. It was Riya who breathed life in him. Smiling with Riya came as naturally as fragrance in flowers.

Riya was his anchor in the turbulent sea of life.

He felt small. Years back, he married someone else because he didn't have the courage to be with her. Even if it was only for the family, but he did. And like always, she did what she thought was right. She didn't marry because it never felt right to her. He never forgave himself for the pain he might have given her.

She always said that the love in friendship is always stronger than any other form of love. She showed it by attending his wedding because she knew it would mean so much to him. He knew she would be broken that day, but still, she came for him.

For many sleepless nights, he cursed himself for being so meek, for not fighting with the world to be with her. He didn't necessarily give up on their love but also didn't fight for it, which, according to Riya, would be an even more pathetic thing to do.

It never felt right with anyone else. He smiled, remembering her eyes when she said this.

He always blamed himself that he wasn't good enough and that she deserved better. Today he realized that he was no one to decide what was better for her. She had chosen it for herself.

He knew what he had lost but didn't realize the extent of the damage until today. Riya was right there next to him, and no matter how much he wanted to hold her and tell her that these years have done nothing but increased his love for her, he knew he couldn't do that. He couldn't just enter her life and wreck it with his feelings. It burnt his heart to take that step back when she was right there. It would have been unacceptable.

But he knew that this was a chance, a chance he should take. He could feel Riya's heart beating when they were dancing. He could feel how he still affected her when he looked at her. He marveled at how adept she was at making anyone love her. Even during the darkest times, it was her smile that kept him going.

He always wished for her happiness, but a little voice always wanted her to miss him.

Riya tossed and turned, unable to comprehend her feelings. She was in Sameer's house with him and his daughter. Even at that moment, she could hear her heart beating. She knew that she wouldn't have been able to stop

Sameer, had he not taken a step back; neither she wanted to. She smiled at the memory of that moment. *He still thinks about acceptable and unacceptable behavior*. Back during their college days, it had taken him almost a year to gather the courage to kiss her. He always thought that she would be mad at him for ruining the friendship they shared.

Riya never stopped loving him. The only thing that changed was the expression of her love. She knew he was married, but what she never tried to find out was whether he was happy or not. She knew it would only make her weak.

She had tried to be in control of herself all these years, but the truth was, she waited to stumble across Sameer in this small town. It felt like they were back to college days where their life revolved around each other.

She almost lost herself today while dancing with him. He has always had that effect on her. She just couldn't help it when he held her and looked into her eyes. There was something about that look that hadn't changed a bit. If only, she thought, the intensity had increased. It now had years of longing and absence that had exponentially concentrated the feelings.

You are acting like a teenager!

She promised herself that she would leave early in the morning before Sameer wakes up. If he saw her, he would know that she didn't sleep, and he would know her state of mind. She knew he would want answers then, and she wouldn't have any.

Chapter 25

Riya woke up to the sound of dishes and laughter, and soft Bollywood music. It took her a while to come to her senses. *Shit! I am at Sameer's place. Shit! I had to leave early.* She looked at the time and was shocked to see it was 10:15 already. She had slept in most of the morning. She couldn't believe her watch. She had never been late. She freshened up quickly and went downstairs.

Sam noticed Riya coming down the stairs. She had made a careless bun, and a few strands of hairs were dancing on her face. *The bun that my fingers untied yesterday.* He shook away the thought. He went towards her and was about to give her a peck and remove her hair when he noticed Anaya and realized what he was about to do. He turned towards the fridge and bent down as if to look for something.

Riya knew the look in his eyes, and her heart skipped a beat. Wouldn't life be simply incredible if this is the first feeling you feel every morning after you woke up?

"Bonjour, Riya!" Anaya beamed.

Riya looked at Sam as he closed the fridge and raised her eyes.

"Bonjour," Riya said slowly.

"Eggs, oats, or cereals, Mademoiselle?" Anaya asked, pointing at the fully stocked kitchen slab.

"Eggs. Mademoiselle?"

"Anaya has taken French for this semester. So, we are practicing." Sam said, clearing the confusion in Riya's head.

Anaya started pouring coffee and was about to add milk when both Riya and Sam stopped her in unison.

Anaya was startled and looked at both of them.

"I don't take milk with my morning coffee." Riya told her. She looked at Sam, and years of recognition passed through.

"Papa, eggs!" Anaya yelled and pulled Sam out of his memory.

"I don't know when he will learn. Eggs are the easiest." She rolled her eyes. "You know Riya, when I was little, Papa used to cut fruits for me. He could cut pineapple so effortlessly without missing even a single thorn. But when it came to..."

"Hey. Anaya! That's our secret." Sameer interrupted, pointing the spatula towards Anaya.

Anaya giggled.

"Hey, come on. Anaya, tell me in my ears, secretly." Riya bent to Anaya's height and cupped her ears.

"He can cut a pineapple so easily, even remove the thorns, every single one of them. But when it comes to just peeling an apple, he always cuts his fingers." Anaya smacked her head with her hand and shook her head. Riya laughed at Sameer and felt an adoration towards this father-daughter duo.

Over a period of time, life doesn't change that much. Circumstances make you adaptable, but your own personality, if you have been faithful to it, hardly changes. He could do every complicated thing even years back, but even the smallest things used to become a task.

Similarly, loving her came so effortlessly to him, yet he was the timidest when it came to just holding her hand.

"So, you both are always this early?" Riya asked, sipping her coffee.

"Mostly. Because we have a packed itinerary." Sameer offered.

"Itinerary?" Riya was taken aback.

Anaya and Sam looked at each other with wicked grins.

"Why do I sense…" Before Riya could finish her sentence, Anaya interjected.

"Riya, please come with us."

"Oh. I don't want to intrude. You both have fun. You hardly spend time with each other."

"No. No. It would be fun. Please! Please! Papa, ask her."

"If you do not have anything important for the day…" Sameer gazed at Riya with deep sincerity.

"Are you sure?" She looked at Sameer, remembering how he loved having Anaya all to himself.

"Yes, yes, we are sure. You adults are so silly. You don't make sense most of the time. I wouldn't have invited you if I didn't want to."

Sameer and Riya laughed.

"Okay, Mademoiselle. But I need to run by my home for a change of clothes."

Sameer felt happy about how the day started. Long ago, this was his idea of a happy family. He always believed that a family that can happily cook together would forever sustain any torrents that life had to offer. Though he had given up on this idea a long time back, he never stopped dreaming of such a morning in his household and somehow, unconsciously, always with Riya. He took pleasure in the knowledge that Anaya likes Riya. He had no idea why it was so important, but it brought him immense relief.

Chapter 26

Sam could identify Riya's home from the far corner. It was the most colorful and green abode in the entire neighborhood. The town was filled with artists, but he had known Riya since childhood. It would be a shame if he could not identify her trademarks. As he parked the car, he saw a small swing made of jute, covered with fairy lights on her patio. *Her reading and thinking corner,* he thought to himself.

He looked around and took in the beauty of her home. It felt cozy and welcoming. The place demanded to be filled with love and warmth.

Hearing the chatter, Mrs. Jennie came out with laundry in her basket. Sameer bowed and gave a flying kiss to her. He was surprised to see a common front area lined with pots. Knowing what Sameer was thinking, Mrs. Jennie offered to tell him how years back they had taken down the wall and lined it with pots instead.

"She is a verbal thinker, your girl!" Sam smiled at Mrs. Jennie. He knew Riya got lost in her thoughts. It was strange how she could think about nothing and everything, and to an outsider, it would seem like a fog of nothingness. It had always bothered Sam, even during college. One minute she was there sipping coffee with him, and the next moment, she was somewhere else where he could not reach. Riya's path to these destinations was only known to her, and the worst part was there was no map to her mind. If you ever tried to trace her ways to wherever she got lost, you would end up losing your own mind. After being together and sharing a couple of lost ways, Sameer knew that there could be anything that could take Riya away from the present, to the places in her own mind, the locations of which there was no map.

He wished he was there when she and Mrs. Jennie shared their lives and feelings. He wanted to know how she felt about things and life in general now. He wanted to sit with her and share her life. It had taken him a lot of time to peel the layers of sophistication and mysteriousness that Riya carried around her like her skin. He knew time changes a person, and with passing time, they grow more layers. He wanted to feel those layers and, if given a chance, peel them off again with the utmost respect.

"Wow! Riya. Your place is beautiful. These pots are so lovely. Did you paint these? Can I please look around everywhere?"

Anaya said in one breath. She was excited about all the colors present around.

"Anaya! No. Bad manners." Sameer warned her.

"No, no. It's okay." Riya chimed in with nonchalance.

"Are you sure?" Anaya asked in anticipation.

"You kids are silly. I wouldn't have said yes if I didn't want you to." Riya mimicked Anaya's voice from breakfast and ruffled her hair.

"You are smart." Anaya chuckled and ran inside as Riya unlocked the door.

Riya fluffed the pillows and hung the keys. Sameer came from behind, taking it all in. He remembered their discussion from years back when they had visited a friend's home. While returning from his place, Riya had carefully observed that a home represents a person's identity and personality. She believed that you would easily decipher someone's persona from every inch of the wall if you look closely. Riya's home was no less than an artist's paradise. Every wall had an interesting and different texture, unlike his bare walls. There were no family pictures but a lot of portraits and abstract art. *Just the way she is, abstract until you look deeper!*

"You did all this?" Sam was in awe.

Riya nodded in acknowledgment.

"You have grown so much as an artist."

Riya smiled as he looked around the place she called home.

"So, what were your plans for today, had we not shanghaied you?" He asked, taking the bottle of water that Riya offered.

"Where do you come up with such words?"

Sameer shrugged, waiting for her to continue, "I had no concrete plan as such. I was planning on painting one of the walls."

"Wall! Which one? Can we all do it?" Anaya jumped with enthusiasm.

"Anaya! You are no Picasso." Sam said, exasperated.

"You know what, it's a good idea." Riya brightened up after thinking for a second.

"What? Are you crazy?" Sam looked at Anaya and then at Riya, bewildered. *They both are mad*, he thought.

"I am not letting you paint, though. We both will do it." Riya said, pointing at Anaya and herself.

"Papa. She also knows your painting skills!" Anaya giggled.

Kids feel happy when they realize that even their parents are flawed and there are things that even they don't know about. Riya realized that Sam probably never hid his flaws from Anaya. She knew every skill his father possessed, which made their bond even stronger. Sam made Anaya feel at par with him rather than a boisterous adult.

Riya brought her painting cans and other stuff from the backyard. Meanwhile, Sam laid some newspapers on the floor and put on some music. Everybody settled and commenced painting the wall.

Sam went to take water and asked for a laptop from Riya. She pointed towards the room opposite the living room. He found the laptop on the desk and wandered his eyes for evidence of her life all these years. He was craving to know more about her life than she was letting on. He found sticky notes stacked on the board in front of the desk. He smiled at her neat and legible writing. His eyes settled on a blue sticky note that had "Don't you dare touch my laptop, Aarush!!!!" in bold and with exclamation marks more than necessary. He felt a tinge of annoyance at Aarush and a grave sense of insecurity that Aarush is a frequent visitor and has more access to Riya than him. He could feel his jaw tighten. He stripped away his eyes from that note and settled upon another pastel green note which had a list titled "WORKSHOP", with all the points ticked. He assumed it would be about the recent workshop she conducted. Another note had a small drawing of a van, listed with things he couldn't understand. One of the older-looking notes titled "PROMPTS" had a list of words, 'fireflies', 'evening sky', 'cacophony of memories', 'home?'. He was surprised at the last one, 'home', which ended with a question mark.

He craved to understand what Riya might be thinking when she was writing these words. He thought about home for a while. *Did she question the concept of home? Or are these just some prompts for ideas to paint?* The more he tried to unravel the mystery behind these simple words, the more he was getting caught in the whirlpool of his own thoughts. He shook his head when his eyes were captured by the vibrance of one of the notes, which were right at the eye level when you sat on the chair. The notes made him laugh, "Stop thinking, you fool." He shook his head and relaxed a bit.

Suddenly he heard Riya and Anaya's laughter. It felt like music to him. He picked the laptop and brought it with himself so that he could work while they painted. The moment he entered the room, he saw Anaya and Riya animatedly discussing something important enough not to pay attention to him. He smiled at them with adoration and started working on the laptop.

They lost track of time. It felt like a family on a weekend, absorbed in doing what they loved yet making sure that they were spending time with each other. Amidst his work, Sameer heard Riya humming the song on the playlist, which made him turn his attention to the view in front of him. And suddenly, the afternoon turned beautiful. He couldn't help but marvel at the two of them. *His two of the most favorite people in the world! How lovely it would be if they could spend every day like this.* A happy and filling breakfast, playing around, then maybe walk around exploring the streets, and ending up on the boardwalk. He imagined going back home carrying Anaya in one of his arms and resting the other around Riya. His trail of thoughts somehow snowballed. He realized that he should ask Riya to go to brunch with them at the French place by the corner. *She would love that place.* And maybe she can enjoy looking at people *if she even does that now.*

"Papa!"

Riya looked at him, knowing he was woolgathering. She had known him enough to know that he was lost in his thoughts, imaginations, to be correct. But life had changed so much. She didn't really know what he might be thinking. But the way Sam looked at her, she knew. She knew he was musing about his life. They had never talked about their future when they were together. But if anything, she knew this was what he had always dreamt about.

Her heart skipped a beat. She didn't realize she was holding her breath. *She shouldn't be knowing what he was thinking. It's too intimate.* Both of them looked away.

"I am hungry." Anaya looked at them, exhausted from all the bubbling energy she had when they started.

"Yeah, me too. Let's go to the French cafe around the street. I love the brunch there," said Riya.

Both Sam and Anaya looked at Riya incredulously.

"Papa loves that place. He says you can sit around the corner and observe people. It's so much fun. Papa has so many games that we play there while observing passerby."

So he does that too, even now. Riya thought to herself and felt pleasure at this new knowledge.

Chapter 27

Riya changed into a floral-print frock and shoes. She covered her head with a hat, and they walked towards the bistro. The waiter waved to Riya. She liked this thing about small towns, the people, restaurant owners, baristas, they know you. It felt good to be a 'regular'.

They sat outside in fresh air and ordered.

Riya was always fascinated by the different lives people led. *Sonder*, a word she deeply felt. Every person who walked on this earth had their own life and people connected to it. Those people, in turn, had their own lives, and more people connected to them with their own set of lives. It was like a prism dispersing several colors. And how little life did they comprehend as an individual? She always felt that we are all caught up in our own minuscule lives that we overlooked how grand this universe is.

She was looking at an old man walking hand in hand with his wife and wondered about the kind of life they must have shared. She had liked the tranquility and purity of this town, but she never knew that amidst the spring breakers, she would meet Sameer. These past few days have been like a dream. Her heart had started beating wildly every time Sameer suggested something, or she felt remnants of past habits still alive. It's beautiful how people hold on to simple memories of people they deeply love. They become absorbed in your essence without you even putting in conscious efforts.

Sam caught a glimpse of Riya. As he had expected, she was looking at people, *or maybe nothing in general.* This was something that always bothered him but made him love her even more. She had the tendency of getting lost in the world of people without being right there. They had spent so many evenings like this. He had always wanted to be a part of her thoughts, but during such times, he felt like a passerby entranced by her serenity.

He could never have imagined that he would experience these feelings again. He never thought he would be that passerby in her life again.

"Let's play our game, papa!"

Sameer enthusiastically agreed and asked Anaya to explain the rules to Riya.

"It's very simple. Papa would ask us a question. We have to look around only once and write the answer on tissue paper. You get only 10 seconds." Anaya explained animatedly.

"Okay. But what kind of questions?" Riya asked tentatively.

Anaya giggled. "You will know. Papa, we are ready. And don't cheat." Anaya gave pencils to both of them and kept one for herself.

"So, how many people are wearing hats that have some red color?"

The three of them turned around slowly and observed their surroundings. Sameer covered his answer while he wrote, making Anaya giggle. Riya enjoyed the feeling it gave.

"Stop!" Sameer called out after ten seconds.

"Riya, you got only one?" Anaya was aghast. She pointed towards a table opposite to them, "Look, there are three girls on one table itself that have hats with red color."

"But that's not a red hat. They just have one red butterfly stuck." Riya argued like a child.

Anaya was enjoying Riya's expression. Kids always revel in the satisfaction when they can correct an elder or win over in a game.

"That's what the question was, 'some red color.'" Sameer winked at Riya and high-fived Anaya.

Riya hmphed, "You vicious people. Come on! Now I am ready."

Anaya checked Sameer's answer like a teacher. "How did you get seven? I got only six."

Sameer asked Anaya to recount the hats. When she was done, he pointed out Riya's hat.

"How can I forget this one!" Sameer locked his eyes with Riya and smiled, making her blush.

"Oh no! Papa, you win this round. I'll ask the next question."

They played a couple of rounds before their food arrived. Riya was having the best time of her life. She rarely felt this carefree. She relished the bonding that Sameer shared with Anaya.

As the food arrived, they dug in and ate in contented silence. After paying the bill, they started walking towards the boardwalk. It was a silent mutual decision. It felt like an unconscious habit shared by them since always.

It was late afternoon, and the day had a lazy tinge to its flavor. They stopped at an ice cream truck to buy ice cream.

Just then, Riya's phone rang.

"Which seasoning you used to add in your fajitas?" Someone asked nonchalantly from the other side of the phone as if it was a part of an ongoing conversation.

"Hi Aarush," Riya said patiently, reminding him of the ever-absent courtesies in his conversations.

"God, Reese! You & your courtesies. I am sure you won't be the person I would call when I am dying in an emergency."

Riya heard him laugh amidst the noise of utensils. "Tell me!" He yelled from the other side of the phone.

"You are in Cuba. And you are asking me for fajita seasoning? I thought that's the only thing you get there."

Hearing their conversation, Sam walked ahead. He had no idea why he was getting angry. Riya had already told him that Aarush was her best friend. He figured he was jealous of the natural comfort she shared with him and also about the fact that she had shared a significant chunk of her life with Aarush rather than him.

Nevertheless, he was upset and angry. He was more upset with himself for feeling what he was feeling.

"Reese! I was just missing you, so I thought, why not try to remember you by cooking as you do."

"Haha! Who would ever believe those lines?" Riya rolled her eyes.

"Reese! Are you telling me?"

She could hear a lot of chatter from the background.

"Italian seasoning, lemon, and black pepper."

"Italian seasoning in Mexican food? You are a cultural Satan. Bye. Love you."

Before Riya could ask how his travel was going and when he would be returning, he disconnected. *Why is he always in a hurry? Jerk!*

Sam had walked ahead of her. She caught up with him.

"Aarush?" Sam asked despite knowing the answer.

Riya nodded.

"You seem really close," Sam said sarcastically as he unconsciously tightened his hand around Anaya.

"He is a jerk. He used to flirt so much. You remember the way you used to…" Riya stopped mid-sentence as she looked at Sam watching her. Sam's anger grew.

"Why don't you go out with him then?" He said, surprised at his own jealousy.

"What?" Riya looked at him incredulously.

"Doesn't look like you are just best friends."

"Sameer!" Riya glared at him.

"Riya, let's go to the other end of the boardwalk. They have a beautiful carousel there." Anaya spoke, finishing her ice cream.

"She is busy, Anaya. We took up a lot of her time already." Sam said before Riya could even open her mouth to answer. He was really furious, and he had no idea why he was even expressing it. They hadn't yet talked about their feelings towards each other, and he had no right to act the way he was. He felt the old instincts come alive, which made him possessive of Riya, but the words were already out in the air, and he could not take them back, not that he wanted to anyway.

"But papa!" Anaya was taken aback by Sam's frenzy. She was gaping at her dad's outburst.

"Let's go." He said, holding Anaya's hand. "Thank you for bearing with us today." He looked at Riya with hurt in his eyes and walked towards his home.

Riya was shocked at the turn of events. She couldn't comprehend what just happened in a few minutes. Everything was wonderful. She couldn't understand why Sam was so angry.

Aarush!
But why?
Oh!

Chapter 28

Riya walked back to her place, baffled.

"What's that look, lady? My plants are going to wilt if you carry that look every now and then." Mrs. Jennie pointed at Riya.

Riya smiled at her. Like a perfect pair of shoes that would fit without hurting your ankles, Mrs. Jennie has always been there whenever she needed her.

"Aarush called."

"Oh my God! You kids! Fought again? Why do you even bother to mind each other?"

"I was with Sameer."

"Oh!" Mr. Jennie instantly knew what might have happened. "Sameer has the right to know, Riya."

"I know. He knows Aarush is my best friend."

"I don't think that's enough."

"What do you mean?"

"Men like to mark their territory. They revel in the knowledge that their woman is wholly and solely their own." Riya looked at Mrs. Jennie. Understanding what Riya might have comprehended, she continued, "Not in a negative way, not like a possession or anything. But they want to know that the woman they love has no one else in mind but them. It boosts their male ego. Though I am not saying it is absent in females." Mrs. Jennie gave Riya a look knowing well enough how possessive she is, "But the intensity of this feeling of possessiveness has a whole new dimension in males."

"But Aarush…" Riya tried finding an anchor in her muddled thoughts.

"What do you expect from a guy who has met the person he loves after twelve years. Someone who knew every second of your day is lagging by twelve years. And then comes Aarush, who is charming enough to make you laugh and has known you for all those years that Sameer hasn't. It's not easy to accept that someone you love is enjoying a similar kind of comfort level with another guy."

"Mrs. Jennie, I am not sure if talking about love in the present tense is the right way." Riya said cautiously. She still wasn't sure what Sameer felt for her. She understood that feelings might have ended their period of hibernation, but whether the present feelings are genuine or just a natural reaction to meeting someone you once loved, she wasn't sure. She knew she affected Sameer even now, and vice-versa but that could be the effect of remnants of their love. The more she thought about it, the more she felt confused.

"A charming guy like Sameer does not get insecure just for anything. I have seen the way he looks at you. He knows what you feel for him, but sometimes, just knowing is not enough."

"You are saying he is insecure? Sameer?" Mrs. Jennie nodded in acknowledgment.

After thinking for a while, Riya asked, "If he knows what I feel, then why? It simply means he doesn't trust me enough."

"Oh, you kids at a tender age! Insecurity is the highest mark of love, darling. Only a person who loves you would be insecure about you. It has nothing to do with trust. It is a basic human tendency to keep what is yours for yourself. Do you let other artists paint on your canvas?"

Riya shook her head.

"Why? Don't you trust the other artist?" Mrs. Jennie continued, "You do not let anyone else paint, not because you don't trust them, but because you are possessive about your canvas. You believe that whatever you make out of the canvass is your personal right, no matter how it turns out to be. It is the same when it comes to human emotions. People who love you aren't insecure because they lack trust. Rather they are possessive about what they feel and what they make the other person feel. It is that trust that makes them possessive; the trust that you belong to them."

"You and uncle would have been so happy. You know everything about men and relationships."

"My love, time and being in a relationship you care about teaches you a lot. Every relationship is different because the people involved are different. You only learn when you keep exploring the different versions of your relationship," Mrs. Jennie turned around to correct herself, "different versions of the *same* relationship." Mrs. Jennie winked towards Riya.

Riya chuckled as she knew Mrs. Jennie hadn't lost her youth in all these years. She kissed Riya on her forehead. Riya felt at ease now, and her mind was a little calmer than before.

"Why are relationships so complicated? Why can't they be simple?"

"If they were simple, everybody would excel at them. There won't be any heartbreak and loss. And if there isn't any heartbreak, a 'Sameer' wouldn't hold on to a 'Riya' with such passion."

Riya looked at Mrs. Jennie, trying to understand what she was implying. She blushed and let the sentence be.

Sam was restless ever since he walked away from Riya in anger. He couldn't understand why he was so angry. It wasn't even like she was supposed to be waiting for him all these years, and now, when he was here, she should leave the life that she has lived and just be with him. She has friends, some commitments, and it was childish to expect her to shed all those just because he is here.

And even if he was angry, he realized that wasn't the way you behaved. He was the one who was responsible for everything that did not happen between them all those years back.

It was a simple thing, but still, Sam couldn't wrap his head around the fact that someone could make her laugh other than him. He should be thankful for her smiles, but here he was burning with jealousy.

It's not even like you kept your promise of making her smile for the rest of her life. Why do you expect her to believe in you again? And why are you insecure if she is smiling because of someone else? Did you want her to wait in misery till you showed up after twelve years to make her smile?

The more Sam thought about this, the more guilty he felt. He shouldn't have walked away like that. He had no right. He was exasperated. He picked up his phone to message Riya when his phone beeped.

"Sameer." It was Riya's text.

His vision blurred, and eyes filled with tears; tears of holding to his sanity that he had found in Riya again. He felt he had lost her once again. *She will never let you lose her, you idiot.* He breathed a sigh of relief and smiled at the text. He knew the feelings Riya may have wrapped in that name. He knew he had to make amends for his behavior.

"I am so sorry, Riya. I acted like a total wuss. I am really sorry. Can we meet tomorrow for lunch, please?"

"Of course!"

Chapter 29

"Hey." Riya greeted Sam, who looked nervous. "Where is Anaya?"

"Oh, she went to buy some stuff with her friend and her mom."

Riya nodded in acknowledgment.

"Sameer."

"Riya."

They both said in unison.

"Go ahead." Riya gestured towards Sam.

"I am sorry for last afternoon. I didn't know what I was thinking. I don't even know why I was angry."

Riya raised her eyes towards Sameer.

"Okay, I know why I was angry. But I also know it isn't my right to behave that way. I am really sorry for putting you in that spot. I shouldn't have behaved that way. I'm sorry."

Riya smiled at the guy who was sitting in front of her. The charmer, the smiling assassin of his times, was nervously fidgeting because he was sorry.

She smirked at him.

"So, Sameer, the charming guy, could also be jealous?"

Sameer straightened his back. "Hey, who said I was jealous. I was just angry."

"Oh, just angry!" Riya teased Sameer.

"Of course, people should respect privacy if someone is walking around with an old acquaintance." Sameer was more nervous and was looking everywhere except at Riya.

Just then, their eyes met, and both their tensions dissipated. They laughed at the absurdity of the situation. Just then, they saw Anaya coming with a bag full of stuff.

"Hey, Riya. Papa didn't tell me that you would also be here."

"Because I wasn't sure Ms. Riya would agree to come." Sameer looked at Riya sincerely.

"So, what were you shopping for without your dad?"

"Oh, I had to buy some stuff for the coming academic year. Papa never comes with me for my academic year shopping."

Riya looked at Sam, who appeared a little sad. She had no idea what happened. He was just now grinning from ear to ear.

"I am hungry, papa. Can I order already?" She said, holding the menu and already reading through it.

The waiter came and took their orders. Anaya excitedly showed her shopping to Riya. Sameer was lost somewhere, and Riya could feel it. *Is he still angry about what happened yesterday? But wasn't he just laughing with me?* As the food arrived, they started digging in.

Riya looked at Sam, who somehow had lost his appetite.

"Are you alright?" She asked Sam.

Sam nodded slightly without looking up at her, staring at the food as if the answers were hidden in the croissants' twists and turns.

"What happened?" Riya was starting to get worried.

"Nothing happened. I am leaving tomorrow for my boarding school. He will ruin this day like every other day before I leave." Anaya said facepalming.

Riya laughed. She knew it was a sensitive thing, but she felt adoration towards Sam. He was flustered with both of them.

"That's why he never comes shopping with me for my academic year. Such a baby." Anaya said, pointing to Sam, who was still brooding.

Riya smiled, looking at Sam for an answer. It is indeed true that no one can understand someone else's feelings because you aren't really able to feel those things. And words, like always, never do justice to the emotions, at least the intense ones.

She was busy admiring their bond when Sam puffed. "Baby? Me? You get busy with your friends and academics, and I am left here alone."

"See. Baby!" Anaya chuckled. "You know Riya, if possible, Papa would not let me go with any of my friends anywhere and keep me with him, always, 24x7."

"Hey. That's because I love you." Sam retorted, mystified.

Riya was shocked at the way Sam just expressed it. Had she heard the same thing from someone else, she would have definitely laughed at how an adult behaved, especially in front of his child. But knowing Sameer, she knew he would be a father who considered his daughter an equal in every way. And that's why he didn't shy away from expressing his heart in front of Anaya.

Riya had started to love the bond Anaya and Sam shared. Sometimes she felt that Anaya acted mature for her age. She knew it was probably because her home dynamics have not been that of a regular child growing up with both parents. And moreover, boarding schools do tend to make you more aware of the world around you. Also, Sameer would have always given her an equal status as an adult.

While Sam was hungrily carving out the croissant as if his answers lay there, Anaya chatted away happily with Riya about her boarding school and the things she is planning to learn this year. As they finished their meal and paid, they started walking towards the boardwalk.

It had become a kind of ritual for them to head in the same direction after every meal they share, without anybody suggesting it—*Like a silent mutual love.*

Sam was walking ahead of the two of them, still sad and gloomy, hands in pockets.

Riya observed Sam from behind. She could never have imagined that the broad shoulders she had seen just a few days back at Starbucks could turn out to be Sameer's. She found it strange that it was at such a pretentious place that caused the stirring of the most real feelings within her.

This man, who made the girls go crazy with his smile, has surrendered to his daughter. She felt a sense of pride knowing him. He was no longer a carefree guy with fleeting emotions but rather a devoted father with responsible emotions.

"Riya? Can I ask you for a favor?" Anaya asked innocently.

"Of course, darling. Anything!" Riya bent and kissed the hand she was holding.

"Can you try to come to our place often and eat with papa? He becomes so busy once I am gone that he skips his meals."

The sincerity in her eyes made Riya's throat constrict. She remembered how difficult Sam found it to eat a meal all alone. She could remember all those college days when he had gone earlier than his friends and used to skip his meals just because he was alone. Habits die hard. Or maybe, habits make people who they are and become like a skin you never shed. She bent down and held her face tenderly and kissed her forehead. She knew he missed Anaya terribly to eat home-cooked food when he knew that his daughter might be managing the monotonous hostel meals.

"Don't worry. I'll make sure he doesn't skip his meals. And next time when you are here, his eggs won't be burnt." Riya smiled at Anaya, and they laughed.

Seeing him sad, Riya couldn't help but walk towards Sam. Their hands brushed a little, and they felt a shiver that surprised both of them. Sam was the first to look away.

She regained her control and asked him, "Do you want me to come with you tomorrow," she hesitated before continuing, "if it's okay with Anaya?"

Riya didn't know if this was within safe limits, but she couldn't see him handling his sadness alone.

Sam looked at Riya with such intensity as if she saved him from drowning.

But the caring father with responsible emotions was a little skeptical. He didn't want Anaya to be with a third person just because it would give him the strength to face the sadness. He didn't wish Anaya to feel that their time together was being shared. The last day was priceless to both of them, and Sam didn't want to compromise on Anaya's feelings. He was about to refuse when Anaya came from behind and beamed, "I would love for you to come along, Riya. Papa would also have someone with him when he drives back home."

Sam was awestruck. The skepticism that he was feeling was shadowed entirely by Anaya's optimism and feelings towards Riya. He whispered a 'thank you' to Riya, and she saw his shoulders relaxing.

Chapter 30

"Papa, can you please cheer up. I am not going on a war. I'll see you again after two months."

Anaya remarked at Sam's sullen mood while on the way to her boarding school.

"I know. I just miss you already."

"Once I am gone, you will be back to your busy schedule. Don't be so dramatic." Anaya busied herself in going through her list for the orientation. She dozed off on the way as Sameer and Riya talked about random things.

"Are you okay?" Riya asked cautiously.

Sam just smiled and nodded. He looked longingly at his daughter sleeping behind with her new backpack.

They reached the main gate. Sam parked his car and took out Anaya's luggage.

"Riya, it was so much fun being with you. I also packed your scarf with me." Anaya smiled at Riya, who hugged her warmly and kissed her on the forehead. Anaya turned towards Sameer, pouting like a child whose chocolate has been taken away, "Papa, now Riya is also here. She can keep you company, and you will be fine. This is like a role reversal. You are my dad. You should be saying all this to me." Anaya rolled her eyes. Sam smiled at his daughter, who had grown so sensible in just a couple of years.

"I love you. Keep writing me letters." Sam bent down on his knees and held her hand.

"Yes. And please improve your handwriting. It's hard to understand your letters."

Anaya hugged Sameer and then turned to hug Riya. Before entering the gate, she ran back to Sameer and hugged him tighter. Sam kissed her forehead and her hands. "Take care."

The moment Riya heard these two words, she was pulled back to the day when she returned from Delhi all those years ago, and Sam had come to drop her off. They had spent two beautiful days together, and the intensity of emotions they both were feeling was impossible to give words to. Riya remembered him holding her hand, looking deep in her eyes, and whispering, "Take care." All these years, it was that moment and the emotions in Sameer's eyes that had made Riya take care of herself through thick and thin.

As she turned to look at Sameer, she saw him wiping off his tears and lowered his shoulder in slight resignation. They walked towards the car and settled back in.

"Every time I drop her off, a piece of my heart dies." Sam whispered, resting his head on the steering wheel.

"I am sorry. I …"

She knew no amount of words could ease his pain. These past two weeks, she has seen how much he loved his daughter. *They really are one soul.* She just silently held him and kept moving her hands in his hair.

"I wish she could always be with me." Sam looked up towards the gate as if Anaya would magically appear and go back with him.

"I am sure sooner or later you will make that happen. You have raised her well, Sameer. I am so proud of the kind of father you are."

Sam sighed and shifted gears.

"So letters?" Riya asked questioningly as they started driving back.

He smiled. It was a habit that Riya had instilled in him when they were in college. She was a letter-writing person. And during all those years they were together, Riya expressed every single feeling through letters. He remembered waiting for her letters in college and then rushing downstairs to the post box to pick her parcels.

The first time he asked Anaya to write a letter was the day it was his birthday. It was one of those days when he remembered how years ago, Riya had sent him fourteen letters, one for every year they had known each other. He was never particular about birthdays or even celebrating them, but he wanted to feel that happiness, the happiness of receiving a letter. And ever since then, the habit never stopped. Anaya had been regular in writing him letters. What started off as a one-time gift that he asked for became an effortless ritual. And Anaya, like Riya, was a great letter writer.

"Yes. Someone I knew wrote a lot of letters. The happiness I felt when I received the letters was like paradise." Sam said, sincerely looking at Riya. She smiled at the memories.

"And she really writes to you?"

"Riya! She is amazing. Just like you used to pour your heart out in letters, she does the same. She beautifully articulates her feelings. Whenever I read her letters, I feel she is right here, cuddled up in my arms," he smiled at the feeling and continued, "though her letters do always complain about my letter writing skills."

"Yeah, I heard that. Handwriting! You still suck at that?"

"Hey! You women are generally artistically gifted, especially when it comes to handwriting. We men do not have the patience to write beautifully."

"What? I can't believe you just gender-biased it." Riya said incredulously. "Have a better excuse next time."

Sam shook his head, looking at Riya's expressions. "Anyway, it is one thing to hear from someone else, and totally different from your own daughter. All those past years, you complained just once, but she does that in every single letter she sends. Every P.S is a complaint!"

Riya laughed. Sam was in a better mood now, and she felt relieved.

He played some soft music and turned to look at Riya.

"Look ahead and drive, Sameer."

"Thank you," Sameer said, looking into her eyes.

Riya looked at him, questioningly.

"For today. For being here. The day I drop off Anaya," he considered before continuing, "is the worst of all the days that follow. Thank you."

"When did you learn such manners?"

"You still haven't learned to take compliments, though," Sam said sincerely.

Riya blushed a little and looked far outside the window.

"Let's have some coffee." Sam offered as they turned towards the town. He didn't want to be alone so soon, and Riya made him feel he belonged.

It is weird how our sense of belonging takes a plunge as our kids go off to school or colleges as if they gave us our identity. You stop being a normal, caring, and loving parent and instead turn into an apprehensive and aching one, always worried about the kids.

"I heard her saying you will be busy now. Is this what keeps you busy? Going on coffee dates?"

"So, this is a date?" Sam grinned.

"You know what I mean." Riya punched his shoulders. "What about your work?"

"Like always, I know how to prioritize. Now shall we? If you are done with your questions."

Chapter 31

They talked about each other's work and perspectives towards life. It was a long drive, and Sameer treasured driving with Riya in the passenger seat.

"By the way, I am officially assigned to look after your meals, not just coffee, so you will have to eat lunch too with me."

Sam looked at her, not entirely understanding what she was trying to say. Sooner than later, he realized Anaya might have asked her to.

"So, she knows I skip meals." Sam chuckled.

"Sameer, she is very sensitive to your emotions. You know how mature she is."

"Ya, I know. Sometimes I feel she grew up too fast. I never made her feel that she can't do something or have something just because she is a child. I always wanted to make sure she felt that she was at par with me. But the way she has matured, it sometimes scares me a little."

"You are an amazing father, Sameer."

"I hope so. I hope to succeed in at least one relationship." Sameer said in a pained voice.

"Sameer," Riya said slowly, tilting her head on the headrest.

"Yeah yeah. Anyway, when did you two talk about me?"

"That's a secret." Riya winked at him.

"Hey! Don't get too cozy with my daughter. I don't want her to love you more than she loves me." Sameer whined.

Riya laughed at Sameer's insecurity.

"What? I am serious. It is so easy to fall in love with you."

Before they both knew the air inside the car turned warm, yet they could feel goosebumps on their skin. Riya lowered her eyes and ended up resting on Sam's Adam's apple, which was bobbing restlessly. She had known this movement so well. She remembered the first time she kissed him while he was driving. She had held his hands and was expressing how much she loved him. Even during that moment, she noticed how his Adam's apple moved, and she knew what she was making him feel. It was then she had gathered her courage and kissed him.

She shook away the memory as she warmed inside.

"Still can't eat alone?"

Sam smiled and let the question be for a while.

"I have had enough meals alone now to be okay with it, Riya. But I feel I am betraying Anaya by eating proper home-cooked meals while she struggles with hostel food. I mean, I know the hostel food is good enough, but you know right, how the food in the mess makes hostelers feel. It aches to swallow any food I prepare at home."

"Fine. Let's have burnt food then."

They both laughed, and the atmosphere lightened. They fell into comfortable silence after a while.

"I can't believe how vulnerable you are when it comes to Anaya." Riya smiled at Sameer.

"Love makes me vulnerable. And there have only been two people who have made me feel that way." Sameer said earnestly, in a low voice that ended in a murmur. Riya swallowed a lump and looked elsewhere. She could feel herself wrapped in the blanket of his voice and laying there without caring for the world.

Sam switched off the music and headed towards his home.

"Where are we going?" Riya got alarmed as he turned towards his home. She looked at him. "Why are we going towards your home?"

Sam let out a laugh.

"I'll park at home, and we'll walk."

Riya nodded. "Oh!"

"What did you think?" Sam raised his eyes and teased Riya.

Sam shook his head and parked his car. They started walking in comfortable silence. It was a little cooler today, so there were few people on the streets. As they approached the French cafe, they looked at each other, surprised. They hadn't decided before coming here, yet somehow both of them walked towards the same destination, *yet again!*

They settled on their usual seat and placed their order.

"Are you still upset?" Riya asked, sensing a little melancholy around Sam.

"Not upset, really, but I wish I could keep her with me like every other father. I hate to see her off to boarding school. That's why I don't like to go academic shopping with her. It reminds me that she would be gone in a few hours." He said, looking far away.

"I am sorry."

"It's okay." Sam sighed. Taking a deep breath, he continued, "Sometimes I think I should have dragged my marriage. At least I would have had the pleasure of being with my daughter every day. Every other pain would have been worth it when I would see her smile."

"And do you think she would have been able to smile seeing you sad and dissatisfied every day? She enjoys being with you because you are happy. Had you not been happy in life, you wouldn't have been able to even cherish her smiles, and neither would she be happy being in such an unhappy place."

"I miss her."

She placed her hand on his and tried to soothe his pain. She had not experienced the pain of separating from a child herself, but she felt a warm connection with Anaya for the past two weeks. If she were feeling sad, then Sam would be ten times sadder.

"Do you remember the first time we all came here?" Sam asked, still remembering Anaya and how lovely the moments were with the three of them.

"After the Picasso stint! Of course." Riya laughed. Their coffee arrived, and Riya poured it for both of them.

"It was so surprising that we both loved the same place yet never stumbled across each other. Isn't it?"

"Destiny." Riya shrugged.

"Always either out on a walk or playing around." Sam said, sipping his coffee.

"But to be honest, more often than not, I imagined stumbling upon you someday." Riya blushed as if she made a big confession. Sam raised his eyes and grinned from ear to ear.

"Really?" he commented, dragging it a little more than necessary. "Tell me more." His eyes exposed the mischievous thoughts playing in his head.

Riya glared at him, still blushing at the unexpected expression.

"Come on. Tell me."

"Fine. But don't pamper yourself." She took a sip before continuing, "So, there were times when I imagined bumping into you coincidentally. Sometimes I would imagine sitting here and hearing your voice from somewhere, only to see you sitting right across from me, talking to someone on the phone. Other times I would imagine you coming to me while I am having a beer and saying 'finally started having a beer.'"

She looked at him, and they both smiled. "But whatever situation I imagined, when we met, we both always hugged tightly." She licked her lips and raised her eyes cautiously, only to find Sameer's eyes boring into hers.

"I would have given anything to get a single hug from you, those big bear hugs you always gave." Sam looked deep into her eyes and rubbed his thumb on the back of her palm.

Riya observed his Adam's apple again and shivered slightly.

She busied herself with her coffee. After they finished, Sam offered to walk Riya back home.

He realized, deep within, he didn't want to let go of her too soon.

They were walking back from the cafe when Riya suddenly turned towards Sam.

"Do you mind if I read the letters she wrote to you?"

"What? Why?" Sam was perplexed, not expecting this at all.

"No reason. Just like that." Riya didn't know why she felt like reading Anaya's letters. She knew how personal a letter is, and this was a very intimate thing to ask. But somehow, she didn't filter her thoughts, and the sentence was out there before she could edit it.

"Are you sure?"

"Why would I ask if I wasn't sure." They laughed as they remembered that this is exactly what Anaya would say.

They turned towards Sam's house and passed several stores displaying hand-made paintings. Riya's pace slowed the moment she checked the displays through these stores. As they reached Sam's house, he started picking up a few dry leaves and putting them in a basket before opening the door. When he saw Riya looking questioningly at him, he cleared her doubt. "Manure."

After a while, they entered and headed to Sam's room. Riya realized that this was the first time she was going to his room. *At least, for the first time after twelve years.* The last time she was in his house, she was so scared that she didn't even let her eyes stray anywhere. She smiled at the memory of that day. It had been just a few days that they had met, and there were so many inhibitions then. And now, in a span of only two weeks, their comfort level was back to the olden days as if the discomfort of the twelve years blurred significantly.

There was a strange sense of belonging when she entered his room. *As if she never left.*

It was immaculate except for the blanket that lay scattered. *He was probably saving as much time he could in the morning and spend it with Anaya,* she thought to herself. As he rushed to fold it, Riya smiled. She knew he was obsessed with folding the blanket after getting up. He had always believed that even if your entire day sucked, when you get back to your room, it would be welcoming and clean at least. He was one of those rare guys who seldom left their bed in a mess.

His phone started ringing. He signaled Riya that he needed to take this call and went downstairs. He wished it wasn't office work. Secretly, he was happy that Riya asked for letters. It would give him a chance to spend some more time with her, especially today.

Riya was about to open one of the drawers when Sameer called from downstairs.

"Riya, I need to urgently go for some work."

"Oh, okay. Let me get my bag."

"What? No. No. I will be back in 30 minutes. It won't take time. There are a couple of books on my nightstand. And when I come back, we can go through the letters you want."

"Are you sure?" She yelled from the landing area, unable to locate Sameer.

"Yes, yes. I gotta rush. See you soon."

She saw Sam leave with his laptop in a hurry, and she headed back to the room. Her eyes settled on his room. She had a heightened sense of being alone in Sameer's home. She felt guilty going through his things when he wasn't there.

Curiosity always takes over the ethical nature of human beings. It is such an essential variable in a relationship. The curiosity makes you say "I love you", wanting to know whether the other person feels the same or not. And it is the same curiosity that makes you go through his phone to find if he is cheating on you.

She slowly absorbed the details of his room, even though there was really nothing much. The wall over the bed was blank. The one across had framed pictures of Anaya and him, playing together, drinking juice at the beach, him teaching her cycling, wearing Halloween costumes, baking a cake. She smiled when she saw those pictures. She had always craved such an unadulterated affection.

Looking at the pictures, she realized how Sameer had made sure that Anaya doesn't miss out on the little things in life just because her parents don't live together. She started seeing Sameer in a new light, as someone who is not only capable, but also responsible towards his relations.

She walked towards the window and opened it to let the fresh air in.

She started feeling hungry and realized that she hadn't had much except for the coffee. *I still lose my appetite when I am with him. Good growing up, Riya. Idiot.* She thought of eating chocolate from her bag when her phone rang.

"Hey, I am sorry. I'll be stuck for a while. Can you do me a favor? Open my desk drawer, the one by the window." She heard Sam clicking the keyboard on the other side.

"Ya Ya, I know." She regretted saying it. *He doesn't know you are breaching his privacy, you fool.*

"What?"

"Nothing, nothing. So, ya, desk drawer, now?"

"There should be a red folder. My passport is in there. Can you please tell me my passport number and other details?"

Riya laughed as he opened the drawer. "Really? You don't know your passport number even now, even after all these years? I always told you to keep soft copies on the drive." She suddenly stopped breathing. She had a flash of their college time when while filling out an interview form, Sameer had panicked as he didn't have his passport, and she had grilled him for not keeping soft copies on his mail.

There was silence on the other side of the phone as well. The keyboard had stopped clicking. She cleared her throat and started saying the numbers.

"You know what, just click a picture of that page and WhatsApp me."

He disconnected the phone. She clicked a picture and sent it to him.

The hunger dominated her senses. She remembered that even Sam didn't eat anything. She went downstairs and looked in the refrigerator. For a single person who skipped his meals, Sam's refrigerator was full of veggies. She took them out and started preparing lunch. Assuming he would be home soon, she set the table and went back upstairs to his room.

Chapter 32

It was late afternoon when Sam entered the house. There were some critical bugs in the network security of the R&D lab, which took up most of his afternoon. He smiled with pleasure when he saw food on the table. He felt warm within. *Typical Riya.* He called out to her. But when she didn't reply, he went upstairs and saw that Riya was cuddled up. He looked at her with immense affection. *She looks so serene*, he thought. He felt a little chilly in the room and noticed that she had opened the windows and the breeze was playing with her hair.

She still sleeps like a baby.

He walked towards her and smiled to himself. She was holding his photo album from Anaya's birth. He kept the album aside from her hand and tucked the strand of hair behind her ears. After covering her with a blanket, he sat next to her, holding Anaya's pictures from her 1st birthday. He turned the pages and realized how much Anaya had grown. He missed her.

Photographs were a strange reminder from the past, of things that were, of incidents that became memories, and of the emotions you carried within at that point in time. He looked at himself in the photographs. He was a proud father, entertaining the kids and being the life of the party. He realized that it was around this time that he used to escape his reality by indulging in such parties where he felt his presence was still welcomed. He made himself feel good through these parties, which made him believe in his existence and that he was still worth it. He hated being just a husband. He had dreams, aspirations, lives to live, and hunger to vivaciously live his life.

Everything that was missing in his marriage, he found it in these parties.

As it happens more often than not, when you try to conform a dynamic person to a particular role, they defy the laws and try to be a rebel; restlessness gains momentum. His wife wanted nothing more from him than being a loving husband who took care of her and his daughter. And as for him, he wanted so much more than just being a lawfully wedded couple and a parent.

And it wasn't long before his wife left him to find her worth in places other than their marriage.

He turned some more pages and found happy faces of him and Anaya dancing together.

Before he knew, the memories lulled him to sleep.

Riya's Diary

19th December 2008

Question your choices when someone makes you feel foolish for loving them too much...

Question your choices when a relationship feels more like a responsibility than feelings...

Question your choices when your definition of happiness doesn't compliment his...

Question your choices when coming back home feels dreadful...

Question your choices when being happy takes every ounce of your effort...

Question your choices when your dreams seem to fade with every passing day...

Question your choices when the darkness of night is your favorite time of the day...

Question your choices when being at home feels lonelier than being with strangers...

Question your choices when you no longer recognize the person you have become...

Chapter 33

Riya opened her eyes and tried to focus. It was dark in the room. The evening moon was peeping through the closed window. As her eyes adjusted, she saw Sam sleeping next to her. She panicked and was about to get up when she noticed his hands were on hers. She took the sight for a moment and remembered every curve and crevice of his face. She had watched him sleep in her lap countless times. There couldn't be anyone who knew his face the way she knew, by heart.

She cherished the peace on his face and how all these years have treated him. She tried to remove her hand from below his, which woke up Sam.

They looked at each other for a while, absorbed in the moment, and smiled at each other. Sam removed her hair from her face and rested his palms across her face. Riya held his hand to her face and let the moment be. It was as tender and pure as the morning dew, and of course, as momentary too.

Suddenly, Riya's phone rang, and they both came back to the present. She got up hurriedly and went downstairs to where she had left her phone while cooking.

Sam followed her downstairs after a while and smiled at her.

"It was Mrs. Jennie. She was worried why I was not back home yet."

"You both seem really close," Sam said, stepping off the last stair and walking towards the refrigerator for water.

"Yes. She has been a golden presence in my life." She said, putting her phone back in her bag.

"There is something about you that makes people vulnerable to you," Sam said, looking acutely in her eyes.

She looked at him, not entirely understanding what he meant. Not in a mood to explain what he meant, he changed the topic and gestured towards the set table.

"So, you cooked dinner?"

"Lunch, actually." Sameer smiled embarrassingly at Riya for leaving her alone for such a long time.

They heated the dishes and sat down to have dinner.

It was after years that Sam was sharing his meal with someone. Not that he hadn't shared a meal, but it is a different thing sharing it with someone you actually want to share it with.

He had dated after he moved here, but after some failed dates and crappy breakups, he had stopped altogether a few years back. He had tried his best to be available to women when he went out with them, but eventually realized that there was always something missing, and he was tired of looking for the missing piece.

They ate in silence. The sound of metal against the china was trying to break the spark flowing between them but failing terribly. Sometimes when two people who care about each other are alone in a huge house, the feelings shared mutually make you feel closer, despite the ample space in the house.

As they finished their meal and started putting the dishes in the washer, Sameer murmured, "Thank you."

Riya looked at him and raised her eyebrows. "Again?"

He came close to Riya and took the dish from her hand, and kept it aside.

"Thank you for making me feel like coming home today. It was a pleasure to walk into a house where food was set on the table and someone," Sam took a deep breath before continuing, "you were sleeping on my bed."

Riya's heart started racing. He always did this to her. His hold was tender, yet something about the way he held her hands made her shiver. She couldn't utter a word, *like always*. Sam came closer and moved his palms to her face, rubbing his thumb across her cheeks. She could feel his heartbeat against her.

The moment stayed there, suspended in time.

He kept looking at Riya, the only girl who had made his heart beat all those years ago, and is still doing so without even putting in any effort. *This girl doesn't even know what she makes me feel.* He hugged her warmly as if he was scared that she would disappear again, leaving him in darkness. Riya's hands instinctively went up to his hair as she caressed him. They stood hugging each other for some time when her phone buzzed.

Riya tried to free herself and turn towards her phone when Sam pulled her hand towards himself. He had no idea what he wanted at that moment. All he knew was he didn't want to let go of her.

"Sameer," Riya said slowly.

Reluctantly, Sameer let go of her hands but held on to the gaze that locked her. They took time to breathe in the reality.

Riya looked away without saying anything and occupied herself in helping Sameer clean the kitchen.

Chapter 34

Back home, Riya could not help but think back to the day that seemed so long but ended too soon. She was in a state of buoyancy. She could feel Sameer's gaze when he had looked deep into her eyes, holding her hands. She was deeply familiar with the emotions in those eyes.

She opened her phone and ended up looking at Sameer's passport photograph. She moved her thumb across his face, his lips, and his eyes. She had always felt the most vulnerable when he looked deep in her eyes. His eyes always expressed more than she could ever handle. She could feel those eyes from the photograph staring right back at her. She felt a shiver run down her spine. Sometimes these unexpressed feelings made her question her sanity. She disliked the fact that she could understand that gaze so intimately. It affected her heart in ways Sameer could never even fathom.

"I will be waiting for you tomorrow for brunch."

It was Sameer's message. The authority in his voice made her feel protected and possessed by someone she has always been in love with. Before she could reply, another text beeped.

"You didn't get a chance to read the letters today."

Oh, so it was about the letters.

Riya blushed at her own thoughts. She couldn't believe how her life had taken a turn. She had blended well with this small-town life and took life as it came. She had settled into a rhythm that brought peace to her life. And now, after all these years of swaying to that rhythm, her life was upturned by rock and roll.

"Well, someone was sleepy enough to waste the whole day." Riya replied, trying to have a little fun.

"That sleep was worth every second."

Riya's fingers stopped moving as she read the message. Her heart skipped a beat as her eyes kept reading the message on loop. She took a deep breath and replied, "Or maybe someone was afraid of being found out that his writing sucks."

"My fingers are meant to do other better stuff."

Riya again caught her breath. She realized she shouldn't have engaged in such a conversation. She knew Sameer was a pro at making her heart race by casually dropping in random comments. *He does not even know how much he affects me.*

While Riya was still trying to catch her breath, her phone beeped again. "What were you thinking? I meant writing codes." *wink*

Riya blushed and felt grateful that she wasn't in front of Sameer. He would have seen her expression and teased her to the end of the world. Suddenly her phone started ringing.

"Hey."

"I just wanted to *'hear'* you blushing," Sameer said in a sincere voice that sent shivers down Riya's spine.

"Sameer!"

"Okay, okay. Did you get home safely?"

"Yes. I have been living here for almost a decade now. I know my way around, more than you at least."

"Well, a guy can't be cautious enough to let a lady like you roam around."

"Sameer!"

"Sorry. Just kidding."

"How are you feeling? The house must feel empty suddenly without Anaya running around."

"I miss her already. This house has never been more alive than it was in the past few days. Thank you, Riya, for making this place a home."

"Well, I don't want to be scolded by Anaya for messing with her dad."

Sameer smiled on the other side of the line.

"You both get along so well. Actually, why am I even surprised? Kids have always loved you."

"I know," Riya replied with dramatic enthusiasm. "But don't be too insecure though, I am not taking her away from you." Riya laughed.

"Hell no! I am coming along in the package! The daughter comes with a father. That's the deal."

They both laughed and talked about Anaya in general. The awkwardness of talking on the phone blurred in the comfort of knowing the voice on either side of the phone. It is strange how you tend to identify the expressions just by hearing the voice of people you love on the phone.

"Okay, Ma'am. Let me be a gentleman and ask you to sleep. I do not want bags to develop under your eyes."

Riya smiled at his words. He had always complained about her dark circles and hated that she didn't take care of her eyes.

"Yes. See you tomorrow."

"I'll be waiting. Sleep well."

Sameer was lying on his bed under the sheets in a happy high state, somehow feeling euphoric. He was hearing Riya's voice on the phone after years, remembering all those late nights when he used to call her to share every little thing.

His mind shifted to the evening they spent together. His dreams were materializing in chunks. He had always dreamt of sharing a warm and comfortable meal in the intimacies of home. He knew the dinner today didn't totally justify what he craved for, but it was like a trailer for the movie he had directed and was shut down due to the lack of actors.

He couldn't forget the way Riya was sleeping peacefully on his bed. *Isn't it strange that she dozed off on the side of the bed that I always imagined being her sleeping side?* He smiled to himself and turned towards her side, moving his hands on the bed where she had lain a few hours back.

He had started to feel his heart again. He promised himself to make sure he did everything he could to bridge the absence of twelve years that stood between them. He was sure of his feelings and somehow felt that Riya also felt the same. He promised himself to muster courage and ask her out officially. He knew he came with a whole package. But knowing Riya, he knew he didn't have to worry about that. All he has to worry about is whether she still wanted to be with him, especially after he broke all his other promises. He hated being the guy who had caused so much sorrow to her, but he knew there was no point wasting time in agonizing over what happened or blaming himself over and over again. God had given them another chance, and he didn't want to lose Riya once again.

He scrolled through his phone album and found a picture of the day Riya and Anaya were painting the wall. It was a candid moment. That photo held his entire life in 2D. He scrolled to the pictures of Riya's workshop and stopped on the one where Riya was laughing over something. He zoomed in and moved his thumb over her cheeks.

I wish I could sleep and wake up to your smiles every day for the rest of my life, Riya. I hope you can forgive me and trust me again.

Chapter 35

The next afternoon, Riya was visiting Sameer to read the letters she couldn't read the day before. She had not felt so light and breezy in a long time. She always tried to keep her mind occupied from drifting to random thoughts. Ever since she met Sameer, her heart had been put to familiar ease.

"Take out the box on the lower shelf. The blue one." He said, folding his clothes from the dryer.

She took out the blue box and opened it. It was filled with numerous colorful pages. She had no idea what she was expecting, but she was thrilled to know. She looked inquiringly at him.

"Anaya likes colors, as you now know. She uses colored papers whenever she writes to me."

Riya was wide-eyed. This was her twelve years back, putting in colors wherever possible, writing letters on colored papers if she only had a black/blue pen.

"Are you sure she is your daughter?" Riya said, teasing Sameer.

"Hey! I am a colorful person too." He said, holding out a red and a yellow sweatshirt in each hand.

"Ya, ya!"

"I'll get something to eat."

Sam headed downstairs to prepare brunch, leaving Riya with the box.

Having Riya in his home gave him an utterly secure feeling. He had no idea why he felt so, but knowing Riya was right there made his heart feel at peace. He had decided that he would talk to Riya about everything today and take a step ahead if she felt the same way.

He called out to Riya and informed her that he was running to the nearby grocery store to get some stuff for their meal.

Riya was absorbed in all the colors with words spilled over them. Letters were a sacred thing for Riya. She believed in the emotions that a single page carried. The writer's words are a part of the heart that he had decided to lay bare. They were one of the most delicate things which were at the mercy of the reader.

She took out the letters and dove into the sea of emotions, not knowing that even the best swimmers can sometimes drown in turbulent seas.

2nd April 2016

Hi Papa

How are you? I don't know what I should write in a letter. But since you asked for this as your birthday gift, I should try. I don't understand why someone would ask for a letter on their birthday. You are so foolish, papa. Sorry sorry.

I miss playing with you. Do you know I am the only girl here who knows how to play cricket? I told our coach that my papa taught me. Everybody was so surprised. I felt so proud.

Okay, take care. Bye.

2nd August 2016

Papa

I love the new painting kit. I will use it for the upcoming competition. I met mummy yesterday. She asked me to focus on my studies and not keep playing around. I didn't even tell her that I am participating. That's our secret. I think she was angry at you.

Does that silly lady from your work still message you? I told you she is dumb.

Bye. I have homework to finish.

I love you.

17th November 2016

Pappppa!

It took me 30 minutes to read your one-page letter. I think you should join a class how-to-improve-your-handwriting. Mrs. Shelly, our English teacher, tells the kids who have bad handwriting to write one page in the practice book. You can also try that.

I joined the cricket camp. Our coach says that if you train kids at a younger age, they will surely excel. But they make us run so much. I hate it. But I enjoy it when we play a match. Did mummy shout at you for sending me the cricket kit? I am sorry.

So finally, you had to block that lady. I think you should become a monk.

I love you infinite.

9th January 2017

Papa

I missed having fun with you this New Year. Mummy's home is huge with lots of furniture. She even has a swing in her backyard. An uncle keeps visiting her. I think they work together. He calls me a 'doll'. It is so funny. Mummy didn't even allow me to have Pizza.

I made friends with Jose. He lives opposite mummy's house. I played cricket with him in his garden. His mom is so cool. She didn't even shout when we broke one of the pots. His dad is so much fun. He did some magic tricks and taught us how to create bubbles from soap. He reminded me of you.

I miss you. Come to meet me soon.

I love you.

12th June 2017

Papa

I am missing you. You didn't sound happy when we talked on Sunday. I hope you are taking care. I am a big girl now. And I can understand when you are sad. Mrs. Shelly says children can identify sadness earlier than adults because they are pure souls.

I want to tell you something. You always said to me that lying is wrong. I did not lie, but I hid something from you. I am sorry. I was looking for my bracelet in the blue box when I found two letters. They were not mummy's handwriting.

Am I big enough to know?

I Love you.

P.S: Can you take handwriting classes!

As Riya read the last lines, her heart flipped.

30th October 2017

Papa

I am thinking about the story you told me. But why don't you tell me the name? I want to meet her. Why didn't you marry her if you loved each other so much? You always ask me to take chances, but you didn't take your chances.

Do you know where she lives? Why don't you talk to her?

I love you.

P.S - It looks like you have forgotten how to hold a pen and write.

2nd February 2017

Paps

I hope your fever is OK now. Did you go to therapy for your back? Our coach says it is important to treat any injury. Otherwise, it may cause more harm.

Now I know why you insisted on writing letters. Sometimes I feel I am more like her than mom. I felt bad thinking this. I love mom. But I think I would be an excellent friend with this girl who sent you so many letters on your birthday.

Yesterday in English class, we were asked to write something about what would be our superwoman moment. Do you know what I thought? I thought that someday I would find that girl, and we will surprise you, and we will all live happily ever after. I didn't write this, obviously. But this was the first thought. I remember you told me once that the first thought we have is always true and what we really want in life.

I liked how she ended her letters. I will be doing the same from now.

I miss you.

Sealed with my bear hug. :)

4th June 2018

Hi Pops

So, nobody knows where she is? This is impossible. You do not have enough resources then. Don't you always keep working on the computer? How can you not even find her? I am sure someday you will meet her just like that in a coffee shop. Practice what you will say. :)

I qualified for the junior cricket team. The school sent a letter to Mom's address, and she was so pissed. She was angry at you too. I told her that the coach thinks I am good and it will not interfere with my studies. I don't think she was convinced.

Are you still blocking those dumb girls from your work?

I love you.

Your eggs were burnt even this weekend.

P.S - Hand is not writing well, I suppose!

Sealed with a warm hug.

29th September 2018

Pa

Yesterday was our movie night in the hostel. I missed watching a movie with you huddled up in a blanket and with popcorn. This time when I am home with you, we should do a movie marathon.

I dreamt about the letter girl last night. Maybe I have been thinking a lot about her lately. She was looking for something. She looked lost. Then I was woken up by our warden.

I hope you mailed whatever you wrote to her and not saved it in the drafts like all the other letters.

I love you.

Sealed with a kiss.

Riya lost track of time as the sun bid goodbye, and the moon peeped from the window. Her vision got blurred, and she realized that she had been crying. She had never thought that Sameer would be looking for her. She had no idea that his drafts folder contained unsent mails to her.

So, we both have a bunch of unsent letters.

Riya couldn't stop thinking. So, when she told Sam she wasn't married, did she give him hope? *Does she even want him to hope?* She was lost amidst all these questions. She knew one thing that they still had feelings for each other. And none of them knew what to do with those untapped feelings. She knew Sameer would be hesitant to take a step ahead, thinking that he is not alone now. She had known him enough to understand how his mind worked. He would be too concerned about her. He would think that he would be burdening her with responsibility. But she knew any responsibility with Sameer would never be a burden. She just had to figure out her feelings for Sameer. Everything else was secondary. She knew she never stopped loving him, and all these past days have been like a fresh fragrance. A little part of her mind always kept knocking, reminding her of all the promises Sameer had broken. But the love she felt for him always silenced those voices.

Chapter 36

Suddenly beneath Anaya's letters, similar-looking handwriting caught her eyes. She pulled out the two letters, and her eyes widened, enough to take in the feelings that were bundled in the curves of the letters.

It was her handwriting. She turned the pages around, holding her breath.

One of the letters was the one that she had written to him when he was about to get married. And the other one was her first-ever letter to him.

"I'll always be there for you; till the time you want me to."

Her heart skipped a beat as this line screamed from both the letters. She drifted back to the past when she always signed her letters with this line.

Though she always poured her sincerity in this line, she never thought she would have to act on these words ever in her life. It is preposterous that when you write certain words, you think you really mean them. But when the time comes to prove the same, you falter and realize how arduous it is to actually express them in actions.

She believed in *forever* but eventually realized that *forever* was never long-lasting, it was just a moment long!

The day Sameer told her about his marriage was the day she realized that subconsciously, these lines used to be the endings for a reason. Those words ceased her existence in his life just like she had promised him. But the heart has its own ways to steer your life. She wanted him to be happy, and without making sure of his happiness, she couldn't stop being there for him.

She didn't realize that it was just a silly excuse to be in his life for as long as possible. It was like those last few minutes you steal after your alarm rings.

And it was then when she attended his wedding and knew it was time; time to step into reality and put a stop to the dream world they both had created. When she saw him entering the ceremony, holding his soon-to-be wife's hand with a smile on his face, she knew that was it. It was at that very moment that she decided to let him go.

It had hurt her for years. Sameer never even asked her to stay. Instead, he asked her to break the contact to make it easier for her to move on. She disappeared from his life altogether, knowing very well that he has someone who is responsible for his smiles and happiness, and her presence would only cause trouble.

It felt like losing one of her limbs. *It still hurt!*

Does it ever stop hurting, losing a part of you? *It never does!* Time never heals the pain but masks it with other challenges life throws at you. You get so used to living with that pain that it becomes a part of who you are, and you carry it with you wherever you go.

Isn't it pitiful for us humans to be so possessive about our pains? We lug it on our backs, within our hearts, and call it 'baggage' despite knowing that we can shed it whenever we want. Perhaps it is a way for us to remember what once was and what could not be—*a silent reminder of the promises you made and didn't keep.* We meet with people with this baggage and expect these new people to understand and even carry the weight around with us. *Silly humans!*

Aren't you such a loser? You read just one line of your letter and look at your thoughts, snowboarding.

She knew she was drowning, yet she did little to prevent herself from soaking in the sea of turbulent emotions. She knew she was possessive about her pain. Mrs. Jennie had counseled her to remember the good moments of her relationship. But the more she remembered them, the more she realized what she lost.

Her old friends had already given up on her a long time ago when she was drowning in the ocean of misery after Sameer's wedding. She had resorted to self-destructive measures. The final blow came on a January weekend when one of her friends found her lying in her bathroom under the running shower. She had to be hospitalized for a week.

A few months later, she received a text from Sameer, asking how she was doing. The text said that though he had decided not to be in contact for her sake, he couldn't let go of the friendship they shared. It was too precious. To Riya, the text felt like a straw in a sea of distress. She clung to it to get hold of reality.

Sooner than later, she realized that the straw wilted and left her gasping for breath again.

It was then that she realized that she should not depend on him to give meaning to her life. She knew he was married and that no amount of feelings, his or hers, can change that fact. He would appear and disappear at his whim since he had his own obligations. And she could not let herself go through the dynamics of a frail heart. *He would never be there to stay.*

And before she made him her weakness, she decided it was time to lead her life on her own terms. She could not keep rowing in a boat whose oars were controlled by someone who was not even sure of the direction.

She left India and headed to the US for higher studies, where she made new friends who had no idea about her self-destructive past. She left behind her remnants like those of a pupal case and transformed into an adult butterfly with wings. She made sure no one found her pupal case with her memories and the person she was. She had come a long way since then. The pain had never subsided, but her perspective towards the pain changed. She realized it pained so much because it meant so much.

Even now, if someone ripped open her heart, they can separate the layers of every pain and struggle that life had made her go through and expose the pain of losing Sameer, who once defined her existence, seated deep within her heart.

She had fulfilled her last promise to him by letting him go. She made sure that she literally disappeared from his life. It was easier after she moved to the US and deleted all her social media accounts. And the best part of living and working in a small town is the invisibility it shields you with.

Finally, after a year of therapy and carefree American life, she realized that emotions shouldn't be taken too seriously; else, they would turn your life into a period drama. She, on the contrary, preferred rom-com.

She never denied the fact that she missed him terribly all these years, and it had taken every ounce of her strength to stop herself from contacting him. Every time she missed him, she wrote him a letter and tucked it under her bed. It was her therapist's idea to let go of her penned-up emotions. She also suggested burning them afterward, but protective about the sanctity of letters, Riya skipped the burning part.

Riya's Diary

25th December 2013

Have you felt your cheeks become hot when feelings well up inside...
Have you felt your eyes water and overflow a stream of tears...
Have you felt losing your happiness while taking care of others...

Sitting by the window, trying not to think...
Of all the feelings I don't want to feel...
But cannot stop my mind from wandering...
Is this the whole purpose of being...
Failing to see the line that separates compromise from the right to be happy...

Those thoughts that hurt the person you truly are...
And not what the world made you...

Snow melts, and warmth caves in...
But Nowhere to be felt in your soul...
For it has been caged in the sensibilities of being a 'good' person...

The music stirs the heart...
And the lyrics ripple those tears in the eyes...
Pushing them off the edge...
Spilling the truth behind those curtains...

155

Alone in this loneliness...
You fight your demons...
Those which you have embraced ...
Believing in the goodness of every being...

Chapter 37

Her eyes again settled back on those last few words of the letters she wrote. Riya's train of thoughts picked up speed as those words screamed at her from the letter. Reading the letters had brought her face to face to the world that she had left behind. She knew she didn't want to go back to those days when she was miserable.

All these days, she was so lost in the pleasure of letting her heart feel sunshine, she forgot the intensity of pain that her heart has felt too. She forgot how far she had come. How can she let herself go through any of these feelings, especially after what these feelings did to her twelve years back?

Riya was unable to wrap her head around all these overwhelming feelings. All the familiarity that was making her feel at peace in Sameer's home suddenly made her feel claustrophobic. Sameer's house encompassed everything that she had left behind in that pupal case. It entailed every emotion that she had buried deep in her heart. It was everything around which she had built her life. It was true that she could not let go of her feelings from her heart, but with time the place that housed those feelings have had several visitors, including anger, frustration, revenge, and betrayal. She never tried to get rid of these unwelcome visitors; instead, she just built her life around those because she knew that there are few emotions you cannot escape no matter how sour they were.

Unsure of what to do, she grabbed her bag and ran towards her home. She wanted to feel the familiarity of the life she had built for herself, far away from Sameer.

As she reached her place, she found Mrs. Jennie watering her plants. Seeing her familiar face, she felt overwhelmed. She ran and hugged Mrs. Jennie from behind.

"What's wrong, darling?"

"Mrs. Jennie." She sobbed, unable to keep her thoughts under wraps, not knowing where to hide them.

It was after a long time that Mrs. Jennie saw Riya in such a broken stage. Whenever she looked at Riya's radiant smile, she remembered the time when Riya was undergoing therapy. She had seen her scared and crying in the dark corners of her home.

It had taken a long time for Riya to get back her smiles and the heart to enjoy life. Ever since then, Mrs. Jennie has been afraid of that black hole Riya falls into every now and then. She knew Riya had come a long way from a wretched and broken young girl to a radiant and confident lady. She knew Riya was as sensitive as ever, and that was one thing that therapy did not change in her, but now at least she knew how to balance her emotions.

Seeing Riya in such a state made Mrs. Jennie all the more protective towards her. She hugged her tight and caressed her hair. After a while, when Riya sobered, she made her sit next to her and held her hand.

"Tell me. I am here." Mrs. Jennie's soothing voice enveloped Riya in a blanket of calm and tranquility. This was the kind of certainty and security that she has earned, not Sameer's home or anything related to him, for that matter.

"I feel foolish, Mrs. Jennie. How can I let this happen? How can I make myself go through the pain again? Why did I let myself be so blind?" Riya was hysterical.

"Riya, what happened? Tell me clearly." Mrs. Jennie was suddenly alert.

"I am so stupid, Mrs. Jennie. Such an idiot!" Riya started weeping.

"Darling, calm down. You were chirpy in the morning when you left. Where did you go today?"

"Sameer's home," Riya said in a slow voice.

"Oh!"

"Why am I so stupid, Mrs. Jennie? Why did I not realize what I am getting myself into?"

Riya held her head in her palms. Mrs. Jennie moved her fingers in her hair, trying to soothe her.

"Tell me what happened?"

Chapter 38

Sameer returned home with groceries and called out to Riya. The house felt eerily quiet. *Did she sleep again?* Sameer smiled to himself, thinking about yesterday afternoon when he found her sleeping peacefully on his bed. It was a simple act, but Sameer felt pleasure knowing that Riya was comfortable enough and did not think before lying on his bed. All those past years when they were together, he always felt that Riya held herself back when it came to asking for what was hers. He would revel in those rare times when she asked something rightfully from him.

He placed the groceries on the table and called out to Riya again. The silence of the house was accusing him of something he couldn't quite remember. He went upstairs feeling a little apprehensive. As he climbed the stairs, he could feel his heart beating faster, but he couldn't place this feeling of restlessness. Before he could comprehend the reason, his bed came into view. The letters were sprawled all over the bed & Riya couldn't be seen anywhere. He knocked on the bathroom door only to find it open. He rushed to the other room in the hope of finding her there.

The sight of those letters was making him worry. It wasn't Riya's way of leaving stuff carelessly outside, especially letters. Then he remembered how she loved the backyard. *She may have gone there. It's lovely weather to be outdoors.* Keeping his thoughts at bay, he rushed to the backyard to find it empty. There was no sign of Riya anywhere. He looked around his pockets for his phone.

He realized he left his phone in the car. As he was going out, he saw Riya's bag was missing. *Did something happen here? How could it be? The gate was locked from outside.* He had installed a security system at home because of Anaya, which buzzed the moment anyone entered other than him or Anaya. He went to his car and retrieved his phone, and dialed Riya's number. When she didn't pick, panic set in.

He rushed upstairs to the room and looked around for any sign of what might have happened. But he couldn't find anything other than those letters. He tried to call her again, but there was no reply.

His eyes fell upon her handwriting. *"I will always be there for you; till you want me to be."*

The feeling of trepidation set in interspersed with constant nagging from his mind.

She ran away.

The moment he heard himself say these words, his legs gave up. He supported himself on the desk and took a moment to calm herself. He skimmed through the letters frantically, looking for any clue.

Please Riya. Don't run away. Please.

He called her again, only to reach her voicemail. He sat there on the bed surrounded by letters. Riya's handwriting was screaming out to him of the coming tornado.

No matter how much he thought, he couldn't come to a conclusion. He had no idea what happened to Riya or what she was thinking. Looking at the sight of the room, he knew that there was something that hit her heart and made her run away.

Did she revisit the past and witnessed the pain of separation again?

He had no idea from where this thought came, but it alerted him. It was like a shot of tequila to the throat.

She is scared.

She is scared of her feelings.

And before Sameer could take control of his train of thoughts, he was pushed to the passenger seat as a mere spectator.

She is angry.

You just cannot barge in her life after twelve years.

You do not deserve her.

His head was throbbing as his mind kept bombarding him with these random thoughts.

She is scared that you will leave again!

Riya's Diary

30th April 2008

I hate you, Sameer!

It looks like I was a pro at fulfilling promises, and you were the opposite. You were always the breaker; the rule-breaker, the promise-breaker, the heartbreaker!

How could you do this to us? How could you not choose us? You couldn't even gather the courage to do what your heart wanted. How could you choose the easy way out? This was all there was to us? Was our bond so fragile?

Why do I have to go through this pain? And why are you the one living happily with your perfect wife? Yes, I always wished for your happiness, but damn it, don't you have a conscience? How can you be happy, knowing the amount of agony you have caused?

Sometimes I feel it meant nothing more than a regular love affair to you. I think you wanted to experience love, and that's what you did. You fell in love with someone who could make you experience the depths of your heart and married someone who could be a lovely wife to you and a good mother to your kids. Because let's face it, marriage doesn't work solely on love. And only love was what we had, no matter how deep it was, in the end, it was just love!

I feel foolish to have believed in your promises. I feel foolish to believe that our bond was stronger and deeper than the norms of society. I was foolish to believe in your sincerity. How did I never see your facade? How did I never see through the perfection of our relationship? I should have known that no form of love can be so deep.

It was like a cloak to the reality of life. I am furious at myself for loving someone so deeply that it pains me to pick those pieces of you now and separate them from myself. How do I find the line where I end, and you begin? I had merged it all. I had lost myself in you, in your love. How do I isolate myself from you now?

Please let me live, Sameer!

Let me be!

Take this pain away.

Please!

Take it all away and do whatever the hell you want to do, with these remnants of our life together that poke me incessantly and make me bleed.

Chapter 39

Riya revealed how the day had unfolded to Mrs. Jennie and how she was taken twelve years back by that one ending line, and since then, her mind has not stopped blaming her for falling in the quagmire again.

She was so absorbed in her tale that she didn't realize her phone ringing so many times.

After a while, when Riya's speech was coherent again, and the sobs could be differentiated from blaming herself, Mrs. Jennie held her hand and looked at her warmly.

"All this because of that one line?" Mrs. Jennie looked incredulously at Riya.

It wasn't what Mrs. Jennie said, but the way she said it that made Riya chuckle. She had no idea why but she felt lighter already. But Mrs. Jennie knew that the past knocks you down harshly not when you visit an old familiar place, but during those warm, carefree lazy afternoons, when you are going by with your life, unaware of the presence of a past, that it creeps in your consciousness, and bang, "Peek-a-boo"! It does not need any significant event to activate the dormant past. An old familiar scent, a ringtone, even just a single word is enough to make your thoughts switch into reverse gear.

"It is not about that line Mrs. Jennie. It is about the feelings I used to wrap in those words. I…"

Riya didn't know what to say. The words that always gave her a sense of peace ambushed her. Her feelings were making her numb, yet again.

"It is about the fact that you never thought you would have to give up on someone who made you feel like that." Mrs. Jennie said as a matter of fact.

Riya looked at Mrs. Jennie. "Yes. Yes! And also, that he would let me give up on him, Mrs. Jennie. I always believed that he would also want me in his life, always, and so I'll always be there."

Mrs. Jennie nodded, understanding exactly what Riya was trying to say.

"Do you still believe in love, Riya?"

Riya was taken aback by this question. She thought for a while before answering. "I think I still do. But I no longer believe that you should expect love to last a lifetime."

"Why do you think so?"

"Mrs. Jennie, when I loved Sameer, I believed in us, in our togetherness. I believed in our future. It was as if I was blind to reality. I strongly believed that love conquers all. I never blamed him for not standing up for us, but I started feeling that maybe our love wasn't strong enough to survive the trials and tribulations of society." She looked at Mrs. Jennie and continued, "Can you believe I started doubting whether my love for him was enough? Don't you think he would have fought had he believed in our love? Tell me, Mrs. Jennie, can you so easily give up on someone whom you claim to be the reason for your existence?"

"Did you talk to Sameer about this?"

"That's the problem, Mrs. Jennie. My words take a back seat when I am with him. It's my heart that drives through the feelings. When I saw him weeks back, it was like a gust of cool breeze in the warm summers of my life. I felt like my corroded heart had finally cleaned itself and started to function. It started beating, Mrs. Jennie. It was like a feeling of serendipity. I was so lost in savoring his presence in my life that I forgot the time when he wasn't there. I forgot what his absence did to me. It was like his presence strongly overshadowed his absence."

"What do you want to do now?"

"I don't know. But I don't want to go through that phase again, Mrs. Jennie. It took me years to be who I am now. You know it very well. I don't want my heart to go through that pain again."

"Riya, my love, sometimes the fear of pain is stronger than the pain itself."

"But Mrs. Jennie, how would it be any different now? I have experienced that pain. Isn't it silly to repeat the same mistake twice?"

"And what about Sameer?"

"Sameer? He already has a life. He has a daughter. How can I trust someone who left me once? Despite the feelings that I have for him, I cannot let him trample upon me whenever he wants. And you know the worst part? Deep within, I know I am not strong enough to resist him, and he knows it too."

"Are you sure, Riya?"

Riya shook her head, not sure of anything anymore. She plucked the weeds from the pots and said to no one in particular. "This is typical Sameer."

"What do you mean?"

"Once, he texted me after a few months into his marriage. He was sorry for whatever he did. Sorry! Can you believe it?" Riya chuckled. "He said he wanted me to be in his life as a friend like we were before we fell in love. He said he didn't want to lose me." Mrs. Jennie gave a sad smile as she listened to Riya. "I was so happy, Mrs. Jennie. I had been going through some of the worst days of my life, and his text gave me hope. And you know how hope makes you imagine. I thought maybe our relationship is not over altogether. We may not be in a relationship, but at least we will be in contact as friends. I was over the top. It was like giving the leftovers to a homeless person."

Riya looked at Mrs. Jennie's expressions. "Don't look at me like that. I know I was pathetic then. I loved him too much to let go every hope."

Mrs. Jennie nodded and asked her to continue.

"So, his message felt like a shelter amidst the torrential rain. I believed that shelter was mine and would be there. But I was so wrong. He again disappeared for months, and I was a fool to make myself believe that he is still there, just a little busy. He again contacted me after a few months with the same thing, saying sorry. I again repeated my mistake and let him be my safe haven, and soon, he left again. Months passed, and I was waiting for his text. The moment I used to think that now I am strong enough and have handled his memories well and that I was doing pretty good carrying on with my life, he would reappear, wreaking havoc. He never stayed, but he never left. And it drove me to madness."

"Oh, darling." Mrs. Jennie hugged her tightly.

"He is doing the same thing, Mrs. Jennie. How can I believe that he will stay? I do not trust myself with decisions when I am with him. He has that effect on me. But I do not want to go through that time, Mrs. Jennie. I want to live my life. Yes, it was a regular life without him. I agree my heart has bloomed ever since we met again. And every time I am with him, my heart sings along. But I can survive without that kind of happiness if it comes at a cost. I … I can't…. Mrs. Jennie… I…."

Riya started sobbing again.

"My girl, you are shivering. Come, let's go inside."

They got up and walked inside Mrs. Jennie's house.

She heard her phone ringing.

Sameer.

Her eyes watered as she disconnected the phone. Mrs. Jennie looked at her but didn't say anything. After a few moments, Sameer called again. Mrs. Jennie looked enquiringly at Riya.

"I am scared, Mrs. Jennie. I am scared of my feelings. I am scared of what my heart wants. It still wants the same thing it wanted twelve years ago. And I don't know how to refuse its whims."

Chapter 40

Mrs. Jennie wrapped a stole around Riya and handed her a cup of mint tea. They sat in silence for a while before Mrs. Jennie asked Riya, "Can I ask you something?"

"Of course, Mrs. Jennie."

"You said he used to appear in your life and leave at his own will." Mrs. Jennie continued as Riya nodded, "Why do you think he appeared in the first place if he had to leave?"

Mrs. Jennie's words jolted Riya. It was like a new perspective in a cold murder case reappeared after years of investigations that had ended in the dark.

But before she could rationalize, her anger and betrayal took over.

"He thought it would be easier for me to get over him if he disappeared. That's why he initially broke contact. And he texted whenever his feelings dominated over his logical self. Because let's face it, I am too good a friend to lose." Riya laughed at herself.

"Do you think he was right?" Riya looked at Mrs. Jennie, not comprehending what she meant. Mrs. Jennie reframed her question. "I mean do you think you would have been able to handle your emotions well had he disappeared completely?"

"What? No! Despite whatever happened, I would have always wanted to at least be in contact with him. I wouldn't have asked for more. I would have been happy knowing that he is doing good in life. He was foolish in thinking that him being out of contact would make me deal with his absence easily. And moreover …" Riya took a deep breath and held up her hands in resignation. "I don't know, Mrs. Jennie. I am exhausted!"

Mrs. Jennie let Riya be. She went to the kitchen and refilled her favorite mint tea. It always helped in bringing coherence to her mind. Mrs. Jennie looked at Riya and saw the little girl who had come to this place with shards of broken memories and lost spirit.

She handed the cup to Riya, who was looking far away as if trying to seek sanity amidst the chaos.

"You know, Mrs. Jennie, when I saw those words written in my handwriting, I realized how life has changed for me. I was this innocent girl who believed in the purity of feelings and relationships. I strongly believed in love. But when he left, I felt everything that I believed in was just an illusion. The truth made everything else we felt like a lie."

"Do you really think it was just an illusion?" Riya turned to look at Mrs. Jennie. "Don't berate your feelings by calling it an illusion, Riya. The moment you label it as an illusion, you remove the credibility of all those feelings you ever had."

"But Mrs. Jennie, had it all been real, it would have been mine, isn't it? He never would've left." Riya asked, looking at Mrs. Jennie, like a child.

"Did you ever ask for it?"

Riya looked at Mrs. Jennie, dumbfounded. She felt as if everything suddenly transformed to slow-motion such that every atomic part of the feelings and the moments they shared seemed to be floating towards her with vividness.

She had let go of Sameer without even asking him to stay, without ever asking him to fight for her.

"Wasn't he supposed to understand that?" Riya asked meekly.

"Now, that is an illusion." Mrs. Jennie said, pointing at her. "Riya, you need to fight for what you love. You need to ask for what you think you deserve. I am not saying that Sameer is justified in the way he acted, but honey, did you really fight for your love?"

"But, what if he didn't want it?"

"Didn't you believe in his feelings for you?"

It felt like someone kicked her from within.

"It has been twelve years to those decisions and feelings, Riya. Don't let those decisions decide your present choices. I am not saying you should trust him blindly or test him. But you need to talk to him. You cannot start a relationship based on past emotions and choices. It doesn't work that way. Twelve years is a long time to transform a person. I know your feelings are pure, and so are his. But you both need to be on the same page, feeling wise!"

"How can you be so sure about his feelings?"

"My old eyes caught his eyes. But love alone is not enough, Riya. If your heart is not at ease, then love cannot hold it together."

Riya kept looking at the tea leaves circling in her cup.

"Sleep it over. There is nothing a good night's sleep cannot solve."

Chapter 41

Sam woke up to the sound of his phone ringing. He felt dislocated for a while.

Riya!

He again heard the phone ringing sharply. He turned around haphazardly, only to find his phone dropped on the floor.

It was Anaya.

"Papa! What took you so long?"

Sam got up and sat against the sofa. He moaned as his back pained.

"Did you sleep on the sofa again?" Anaya warned from the other side of the phone. Sam was still muddled. *Why was he sleeping on the sofa?*

"Papa!" Anaya yelled from the other side. Sam sat up completely awake, aware of the reality.

"Hey, darling. Hey!" He said, rubbing his eyes and straightening his back.

"Are you okay?"

"Yes. Yes. I am supposed to ask you that, not the other way round. You sometimes make me forget that you are just eleven."

"Age is just a number, papa."

Sam rolled his eyes at his daughter's words of wisdom.

"Stop rolling your eyes. Someday they will go inside your brain." Anaya chuckled at her thoughts.

Sameer let out a laugh. He loved what he shared with Anaya. She wasn't just a daughter for whom he was responsible; she was his confidante, his partner in crime, his movie-date, his love! He knew she had a maturity contrary to her age, but that didn't mean she had lost her childhood.

Sam sat straight on the sofa and pulled a cushion on his lap. He suddenly realized it was a weekday, and the hostelers were not allowed to call home on weekdays. Sam instantly knew his daughter broke some rule, again.

"How are you, my princess?" Sam asked, yawning.

"I am good. The principal here might not be." Anaya said casually.

I knew it!

Sameer could imagine her rolling her eyes. He smiled at the memory of his precious daughter and how strongly she felt about absurd rules and regulations.

"What did you do this time?" Sameer tried to sound strict but failed considerably.

"Just skipped a few classes to play Cricket."

"Anaya! Again? They will remove my name from the first person's contact list if you keep repeating it, and I let it go casually."

"Papa!"

"It would serve you better if they called your mom." Sameer chuckled. He got up and went to the refrigerator to get water.

"Papa, it's not funny."

"Anaya! I will only come and meet your principal if you promise not to skip classes ever again. Else I am not coming. Let that nose-hair lady take disciplinary action." Sameer tried to stifle a laugh remembering her principal.

"Promise! Promise! See, at least I will be able to meet you before the next break."

He couldn't help but feel insignificant. Maybe it is his fault that Anaya rebels sometimes. He brooded over his thoughts. But listening to Anaya's voice eased his demeanor a bit. She was right; it would be a chance to see her again, though not a good reason, but still! Anaya hung up the phone after informing him of the day when the principal was expecting him.

He opened his call log to make a call to his colleague to inform him of his leave. As he opened the log, the endless calls to that one name screamed from the screen. *Riya!*

He remembered he was waiting for Riya to revert his calls and messages the whole night. But she neither picked his calls nor replied to any of his messages or voicemails. He scrolled through the call log and voicemail again just to be sure he didn't miss a call from Riya, only to find just outgoing calls.

Lost in his thoughts, he cleaned the trash and headed to the kitchen, and brewed a pot of coffee. He called his colleague and left a message on his voicemail when he didn't pick. He had started to worry. It was highly unlike Riya not to respond to his calls or texts.

He took a bath and checked his emails. The pending work had been increasing ever since the spring break, so he decided to finish it all tonight. But before that, he needed to visit Riya and make sure she was all right.

He had been obsessively checking his phone. There was still no message from her.

Just when he was about to leave to meet Riya, his phone rang. It was his colleague reverting the voice mail. They talked for a while when his colleague asked him to finish a few codes so that he could work on those when Sameer was on leave.

Sam sighed. He again left a message on Riya's number and headed to his study to work.

Sameer's Diary

28th March 2013

Riya

Can I start by saying sorry?

You were right, Riya! It isn't just enough to hear what your heart says. You should have the courage to follow it. It seems after not following my heart all those times; it has ceased to even feel. My heart is numb. If at all, it just makes me feel your absence with every beat.

I knew those decisions would cause havoc, the repercussions of which will haunt me throughout my life. I wish I had the courage to follow my heart. I cannot even start to imagine what you might have gone through and maybe are still going through. If I even stop for a second to give it a thought, the pain it causes becomes unbearably intense. I know being sorry would never be enough to mend what I have done to us.

I had a choice, and I chose the easy way out.
I ruined us.
I ruined my existence.
I ruined the reason I loved to live.

Since you haven't contacted me all these years, I know you must be really pissed off with me. And I would be a fool to even expect you to forgive me for wrecking the togetherness we shared. Maybe the vast expanse of loneliness and misery that my soul is wallowing in is my punishment for causing this disaster.

I know I cannot change the decisions I took. No matter how much I wish we could still be 'us', I know it's all just wishful thinking. I know I lost you. I know I lost my soul when I gave up on you.

Sometimes I feel that I cannot look into my own eyes in the mirror because of the terrible disappointment I might have been to you.

I know you might have questioned my love for you. You might have questioned the bond we shared. I am sorry, Riya. I know it's irrelevant to express how pure those feelings were and that for all those moments, you, Riya, were the reason my soul was in bliss.

My life is a repentance blog. Asking for your forgiveness feels like a cowardly act. I should be going through everything I am going through, for all the pain I have caused you. Asking for your forgiveness would be an easy way out of this misery. And I do not want to choose an easy way out again. I sincerely hope that wherever you are, you are 'living' and not just surviving. Thinking about your smile gives me the strength to be a better person, someone who deserves to be with you.

Sometimes I wonder,
whether you trusted someone again...
whether you believed in promises again...
whether you still believe in 'forevers'...

I wonder, and I hope ardently that you still do! It is your faith that makes you who you are, Riya. I sincerely hope I didn't make you lose yourself.

I am sorry!

Chapter 42

Riya was sitting cross-legged outside on the porch. She had spread out papers on the floor and had placed the paint cans over them. She had switched on her old college playlist and was busy painting the pots. She had followed Mrs. Jennie's advice and slept on her tumultuous mind and woken up with not a solution, but at least an acceptance of the turbulence.

Mrs. Jennie came out with her laundry and was surprised to see Riya immersed in colors, a sight she always loved.

"Looks like a pretty colorful morning, darling."

Riya smiled at Mrs. Jennie and waved her hand.

"There is nothing that colors can't beat."

"They beat you." Mrs. Jennie came forward and rubbed the paint off Riya's nose.

"Mrs. Jennie. Do you still have that Pineapple cheesecake?"

Mrs. Jennie smiled with adoration. There was no feeling better than someone asking for the cake you baked.

"Of course, my love. I will get it for you."

"And your mint tea too."

Mrs. Jennie laughed and went inside. She knew Riya was trying to be upbeat. It was completely like Riya to distract herself when she was confused with reality. *At least she has entered the acceptance phase.*

Mrs. Jennie heard her phone ringing. As she picked it up, she saw it was Aarush.

"What's wrong?" Mrs. Jennie asked skeptically.

"Why so serious?" Aarush chuckled from the other side.

"You never call me. What is it?"

"Are you jealous that I always call Riya? You will always be my first love." Aarush always enjoyed teasing her.

"Mrs. Jennie." Riya called out from outside.

"Is it Riya? Why is she not picking my calls?"

"Oh! Is that why you called me?" Mrs. Jennie said in an accusatory tone.

"No. No. I was just asking. Is she in one of her phases again?"

Mrs. Jennie sighed. "I don't know. I can't understand this girl. She thinks she is so strong and mature. But her heart is still very sensitive and naive. Plus, she forgets that it's her heart that defines her and controls her."

"You guys should not be left without my supervision. Such dramatic lines! Do you even know what you mean?"

"Shut up you nomad. Why did you call?" Mrs. Jennie started preparing tea while listening to Aarush.

They talked for some time before Mrs. Jennie took the cake and tea outside to Riya.

"Who was that? Aarush? What did he want from you? That jerk!"

Mrs. Jennie laughed and ignored her questions. She picked up the paintbrush and started painting.

"Mrs. Jennie. Wait." Riya got up and went inside to get a stool for Mrs. Jennie.

"Here. Do not over-exert your knees."

Mrs. Jennie smiled, took the stool, and started painting.

"So, did you sleep well?"

Riya nodded as she continued to paint.

"You cannot always run away, my love. You need to face your fears."

Suddenly Riya's brush stopped midway.

"I know you are trying to distract yourself. But this is just escaping reality. It is like turning away your head from a fire, thinking it will not burn you just because you aren't looking. And you know there will be some damage, if not anything, sooner or later the heat will catch up."

"He called me so many times," Riya said slowly.

"And?"

"I don't know what I want."

"Take your time. Just do not run away. Face it. You are stronger than you were twelve years ago."

They got busy with painting the pots. Riya headed inside to get water when she noticed her phone beeping. She went to check and saw Sam's text saying he would be coming over to see her.

Riya suddenly panicked and went outside to tell Mrs. Jennie.

"Mrs. Jennie, please. I need some time to understand my own feelings. You do not dive in a pool without knowing how to swim and not even having a tube with you."

"What an analogy, Riya." Mrs. Jennie chuckled. "Why don't you reply to him and tell him not to come?"

"I know him. He would not be satisfied with my reply and would either ask me to come or would come anyway."

"What? I never thought he would be that kind of a guy. He seemed like a very secure person when it comes to girls. I didn't know he was so unrelenting." Mrs. Jennie said airily.

"I always replied to his calls or texts. Always!"

"Oh! Now I get why he is so restless. Woman! You are driving him to the edge. Figure out your feelings before something splatters, and one of you burns in your own desires."

Riya nodded, switched off the music, and placed the pots in direct sunlight to dry.

Chapter 43

Sameer didn't realize when the sun went overhead. The bugs had been creating havoc, and it took him and his colleague hours to identify the problem and correct it. He was hungry. In a hurry to meet Riya, he had just had coffee in the morning and then the phone rang. And since then, he had been busy with work.

He thought of picking something on his way to Riya's home.

Riya still hasn't replied back. Somehow it had started to get on his nerves.

He picked something to eat on his way to Riya's place. It looked so vibrant. He could see the newly painted pots drying in the sunlight. Suddenly he felt angry at Riya. *She had time to paint the pots but no time to reply.*

She is distracting herself, you fool! Shit! I messed up something!

He calmed himself and parked the car.

As he was about to ring the doorbell, Mrs. Jennie stepped out to pick her pickle jars.

"Oh hey, Mrs. Jennie." He waved at her.

Mrs. Jennie faltered as she heard his voice. She was feeling bad for Sameer. But she also knew Riya needed time and her love for Riya was beyond anyone else. She smiled at Sam and asked what brought him here.

"Is she home? I have been trying to call her since yesterday, but she is not replying." Sameer asked, pointing at Riya's door.

"She must be busy with something." Mrs. Jennie gave him a cursory look.

"Yeah, that could be. I was just worried if something had happened."

"I am sure everything is fine, honey." Mrs. Jennie said with a little more conviction in her voice.

He wasn't convinced and knocked on her door again. To his dismay, the door remained unanswered, just like his calls.

"She may have gone out for some work. Why don't you come inside and wait here for a while?"

Sameer looked at the unresponsive door. Unsure of what was happening, he followed Mrs. Jennie inside her home. He looked around and was shocked to see the number of paintings that hung on the walls. Every inch was covered with compelling art forms or some vivid portrait.

"I was an artist myself. Some of this is Riya's. Some are from the workshop Riya organizes. Sit. Make yourself comfortable. I will get you tea. Any particular flavor that you like?"

"Mint."

Mrs. Jennie stopped for a second, hearing Riya's favorite flavor. Sam suddenly realized he might have acted overbearing.

"Umm... I am sorry. Anything is fine."

Mrs. Jennie hurried inside and prepared tea for the two of them. She wondered if both these silly people, Sameer and Riya, really loved mint tea or if one of them made a habit out of the other one's taste.

Sam was still thinking about Riya. He checked his phone to see if there were any messages, but he was disappointed to find none. It felt a little strange to be right next to her home and still not be able to see her. This is how our heart finds solace. We try to stay connected to someone we love by adopting their habits and rituals. It's just a human way of being in the presence of the other soul.

As Mrs. Jennie served him tea, she talked about when she used to create art from scraps. She told Sam that she even used to own an antique shop that organized biannual workshops and exhibitions.

"No wonder Riya's workshop seemed so perfect. A professional was backing her up." Sam said, impressed with Mrs. Jennie.

"I won't take the credit for that. Your girl has an innate flair to organize things and make sure they come out beautiful."

They talked some more about random things when Sameer realized that it had been really long, and Riya was still not back. He thought of leaving when Mrs. Jennie asked, pointing at the bag,

"Is that lunch?"

"Oh. Ya. I thought we could have it together." Sam said consciously, pointing towards Riya's home.

"Do you mind sharing it with another beautiful lady?" Mrs. Jennie said, lifting her chin up.

Sameer laughed.

"It will be my pleasure to share lunch with not just any other beautiful lady but a divine one too."

Sam took her hands and kissed them.

Mrs. Jennie laughed and got up to bring the dishes.

"Why do you look so lost? She must be busy somewhere. Relax!"

"I am just not getting a good feeling," Sam said, agitated with the turn of events.

"Oh, Boy! A girl never stood you up before?"

Sameer looked horrified. *Did Riya stand him up? Did she just break contact with him?*

Serves you right, Mr.!

Looking at his expressions, Mrs. Jennie shook him to the present.

"Relax! I am not saying she stood you up. You got to be in a relationship first." She laughed as if enjoying the slow torture of Sameer. "She might be busy. She has the habit of running around randomly for some work."

"She never leaves my calls and messages unanswered. I..."

"You still have to catch up the distance of twelve years, honey." Mrs. Jennie said promptly, yet in a warm, protective tone.

Sameer looked up at Mrs. Jennie, realizing she was right. The Riya from twelve years ago was the one who always replied to him. He had just assumed that she was the same even now. He felt foolish at whatever he had been feeling since yesterday.

"Mrs. Jennie. Can I ask you something?" He hesitated a bit as Mrs. Jennie nodded. "Is she in a relationship with someone?"

Mrs. Jennie tried to control her laugh but couldn't. She guffawed at his insecurity. She couldn't believe that Sameer was feeling so anxious. It was true how strongly love makes you feel your emotions. It can make you feel belonged to someone, and at the same time, insecure too.

"She would be able to answer that better. But didn't you both spend time together all these past weeks?"

"We did! That's why I felt that we are still at the same place where we were twelve years back. But I just realized that I might be wrong."

"How can you be at the same place after twelve years, Sameer? Neither you nor she is what you were back then. How can your feelings be the same? Isn't it harsh to expect that people won't change in your absence?" Mrs. Jennie sounded more accusatory than she had wanted to.

"No. Of course not. People change. I also changed. But feelings? They may change the form, but true feelings never leave your heart." Sam continued, his voice barely a whisper, "She always believed in *forever*." His voice tugged Mrs. Jennie's heart.

She suddenly felt that they both were deeply committed to each other without either of them realizing it.

"Have faith if you believe in her so much. It takes some time to hit the play button on the emotions after being on pause for twelve years. And if you want my advice, try to remember why you hit the pause button in the first place and whether you are really ready to play the next track."

Mrs. Jennie tapped his hand and smiled. Sameer understood what Mrs. Jennie was trying to say. He needs to give some time to Riya without being insistent. *It is true. She needs time to accept my presence in her life and, moreover, believe that I will always be here.*

Sam hugged Mrs. Jennie and kissed her on her cheeks before he left for his home.

He looked at Riya's house before leaving, trying to soothe his chaos, and left a note stuck on Riya's door.

"I am really sorry. Please give us a chance. Have lunch with me tomorrow."

Riya was jittery the whole time she knew Sameer was at Mrs. Jennie's home. A part of her felt bad for Sameer, but she knew she couldn't rush her feelings, not again.

The moment she felt Sameer had left, she went to Mrs. Jennie and knocked on her door.

"Did he leave?"

Mrs. Jennie nodded. They sat together for a while, soaking in the beautiful colors of the sunset.

"Give him a chance."

Riya looked at Mrs. Jennie, unable to believe her ears.

"Not for him, for yourself. You deserve a chance, hun. Give yourself a chance." Mrs. Jennie said sympathetically.

They sat there for a while, relishing the peace and quiet. Riya lifted the pots they had left to dry in the morning and placed them back.

As she was stepping back inside, she saw the note that Sameer had stuck on her door. She smiled at the familiarity of the handwriting. She moved her fingers over the words written as if she could touch Sameer's fingers when he wrote them. *At least it's legible, unlike your feelings.*

She went inside and texted Sameer.

Mrs. Jennie is right. It's time I should face my fears.
Moreover, Sameer should face my emotions.

Chapter 44

Sameer was ecstatic ever since he received the reply from Riya. He had not stopped reading it. Love makes you go crazy. You try to find hidden feelings even in the simplest of words. No wonder flowers look more beautiful and sunsets holy. Every regular thing starts having a new dimension.

He was nervous as he got ready. He had no idea why he was feeling so anxious. Just a few days back, they had been meeting and sharing meals. But Sameer had a hunch that this meal is gonna be different.

He went early and sat on a curbside table. He was lost in his thoughts when he saw Riya walking towards him. There was a sense of fierce determination in the way she walked. He got up and started to hug her, but something stopped him midway. He gestured to her to sit.

There was a palpable silence for a while before Sameer broke the tension.

"Were you busy these two days?"

Riya looked at the skeptical figure in front of her. *Speak your heart out today, Riya.*

"Not really. I just wanted to think a few things through."

"So, did you?" Sameer asked cautiously.

Riya nodded slowly, fidgeting with her fingers.

"I came to your place yesterday."

"Yes. Mrs. Jennie told me."

Sameer was getting more anxious with Riya's terse replies. He was unable to understand what he did to deserve such a reaction.

"Where did you go that day?"

"I… I had some urgent work."

"I know when you lie, Riya. Twelve years didn't change that fact."

"What do you know?" Riya snapped back at Sameer, who was disconcerted with her reaction.

"What?"

"How is Anaya?"

"She is doing good. She called me yesterday, assuming that you would be with me."

"What makes her think so?" Riya said a little more sarcastically than she meant to.

"Riya! What's wrong? Why are you being so defensive? She just wanted to tell you that everyone loves your scarf. She wears it every Friday to her casuals break."

Riya nodded along, trying to calm the storm erupting in her mind. She had no idea why she was so angry. In the morning, she felt she was calm and in a better state to handle this lunch. But nothing was going the way it was supposed to.

I will piss him off, and there goes my second chance.

So? Is this how you want to have your second chance?

Like a beggar?

Who's being a beggar? But being rational is important.

You are being rational. And a little dollop of irrationality in front of the man who claims to love you is challenging.

Ya, we will see that.

"Riya! Riya!" Sameer shook her to the present when he realized that she was mindlessly adding milk to her coffee. "Can we please be adults and talk it out. What's bothering you? Why did you run away that day? And then you didn't even reply to my calls or messages."

"Why am I obligated to reply to you, Sameer?

"What?"

"What what? Why should I always be available for you? Why am I expected to reply to you promptly when you yourself go marrying someone else?"

"What?" Sam was horrified at what she said.

Riya realized too late what she just spoke. She covered her mouth, realizing the mistake she made. *And there goes your second chance.*

"I… I am sorry. I didn't mean that. I… I was just…. I… it's just that I have my own choice. I should not be expected to do something just because it's you." Riya knew she was losing her facade of acting tough. Her voice slowed to a murmur. She realized she was just picking on him now.

"Hey. Hey! Look at me. Please don't be sorry. At least your anger would make me feel less guilty for making you go through all the pain alone. I have no excuse for what my absence has made you feel. I know I was the one who was at fault when I married someone else, like you said. And believe me, I have regretted that decision all these years." He bent towards Riya and tried to hold her fidgeting fingers and convey the sincerity of his feelings. "You aren't expected at all to do something just because it's me. You have done enough for me, Riya. I was just worried. When I came back home that day, I found all the letters scattered along the bed and you weren't there. And you weren't even picking my calls or replying to my messages. I… I was just restless. I just wanted to be sure everything is okay."

"And do you think it is? Okay?"

"No. Not at all. I can clearly see that something is bothering you badly, and you are trying to fight it. Please tell me what you read that day that made you run away, Riya."

"I just realized how foolish I am to want to throw my life away again."

"What do you mean?" Sameer said cautiously.

"What I mean is, Sameer, how can I trust you with my feelings…" Riya breathed before continuing, "again?"

"What?" Sameer sat up straight, holding his breath.

"All these days, I was feeling like spring. I was basking in your presence in my life again after so many years. For a while, I forgot what I went through when you left. I cannot make myself go through it again."

Sameer suddenly felt as if he was struggling to float even in waist-deep water.

"What if I say I am here to stay?" Sameer says gingerly, knowing that everything that he said right now had the power to make or break his life.

"That's the point. How can I believe in something you promised me years back too and didn't fulfill?"

Sameer felt a hollow in his chest as if someone had pulled out all its contents and thrown it as garbage.

"Riya. Please don't do this. That was different. I was helpless."

"No, Sameer. You were not! You made a choice! You made a choice, and I wasn't it."

"Riya. Please… I…" Sameer knew he was breaking from inside. The hollows were crunching his strength, more so his faith.

"You know, whenever I used to talk to you then, I always felt that time was running out, and you would leave soon. I was never at ease. Somehow my heart knew you wouldn't stay even though you always promised. And yet, I let myself flow with you. I should have known that it won't last, no matter how much I wanted it to. Because you were so casual about it."

"What? Casual? Are you kidding me? How can you doubt those feelings, Riya? It was nothing but the truth. Yes, I know things didn't turn out the way we wanted but even then, what we shared was very much real."

"If it was real, why didn't you ever make an effort to be with me? Do you even know what I went through? And I am not saying only I went through heartbreak or a bad phase in life. I am sure it would have been difficult for you as well. But that was your choice. It wasn't mine. If you suffered because of your own choice, then you cannot blame anyone. You were responsible for yourself."

"I never blame anyone but myself, Riya. I can never forgive myself for letting you go. I always regret that decision I made. My guilt never leaves me alone. And that is why I have been looking for you all these years."

"Why? So that you can ease off your guilt?" Riya snapped.

"No! Because we deserve a chance together."

Before Riya could speak, her phone started ringing. It was Mrs. Jennie, asking her to come home as soon as possible.

"I need to go."

"Can we at least walk together?"

Riya shrugged nonchalantly as they paid the bill and walked towards her home.

* * *

The moment they turned around the edge of their common porch, Riya saw an unruly mess of hair.

"Aarush!"

Riya ran towards him and gave him a tight hug.

"Damn, you are still too hot for me." Aarush grinned as he hugged Riya tightly. "Oh, I missed you, Reese."

"Why didn't you tell me he was coming, Mrs. Jennie?"

"He wanted it to be a surprise."

"Oh, so that is why you called her yesterday." Riya punched Aarush, suddenly feeling light-hearted as if all the tension from the previous conversation dissipated in Aarush's warm embrace.

"Mom was saying you have lost your mind again! And who better to fix it than me. Who played with this fire, by the way?" Aarush said, raising his eyebrows towards Sam, who was standing like an outsider, unsure whether he should cross the line of their happy faces.

"Sameer, this is Aarush, my best friend." Riya reluctantly introduced them to each other.

"And her guilty pleasure!" Aarush said, teasing Riya.

"Aarush!"

"Aarush!"

Mrs. Jennie and Riya yelled at him again. Sam coughed as his discomfort rose.

"Mom, why do you both miss me so much when all you guys do is yell. I tell you, Sameer, women are insane creatures!"

"You are Mrs. Jennie's son?" Sameer says slowly, unable to comprehend the dynamics that were laid bare in front of him.

"I know she looks too young to have a charming son like me." Aarush said warmly as he kissed Mrs. Jennie and let his hands rest on her shoulders. Sam smiled uncomfortably. His mind was reeling to all the times when Riya had mentioned Aarush. *Did he miss something?*

"Hey, come inside Sameer. Why are you standing there? Have some tea with us. I do not mind sharing my two ladies with you for a while."

"I... I should leave." Sameer said, looking at Riya.

"What? Are you afraid of her? Don't worry when I am here. I know how to tame this fluttering butterfly."

"Sameer, ignore every single word that spills from his mouth. He stopped being in his senses right after he left Mrs. Jennie's womb." Riya says, pointing at Aarush's head. "Mrs. Jennie. Are you really sure you didn't pick this brat from trash somewhere?"

"Ha-Ha. How can you crack the same joke for six years?" Aarush said, flicking her forehead.

Sameer's Diary

13th November 2012

People often keep cheering you up, giving you faith that this too shall pass. And you being the upbeat person you have always been, keep finding pleasure and hope in everyday little things. Rather than focusing on what you lack, you always and **'consciously'** thank God for the blessings you have. But subconsciously, you know that God may be grateful, but life isn't, not always. You keep telling yourself day in and out all those chin-up lines you had told people when they needed to hear those. But you eventually tire out of motivating yourself. After all, there is a limit to how much a person can push his own self. Even the best swimmers tire in a sea of crashing waves, especially when the shore is nowhere in sight.

You are drained of your inner energy, drained of the excitement that life once held. You are tired of living your own belief that life is worth every moment. You have been consciously trying to find life in all the moments, the slow ones, the intimate ones, the emotional ones, the lazy ones, the let's-do-something-big ones, the lets-just-watch-NetFlix ones, the crazy ones, the adventurous ones, the spontaneous ones. But now, you are just so tired of trying.

It's not like your life has become a whole bunch of dried flowers. In fact, people keep telling you that you inspire them. But what about your own lost inspiration? Maybe for once, you want to lead a regular everyday life, with a to-do list of things you want to do, not just need to do. Maybe you are tired of just sustaining and not living. Even a candle wears out after sustaining in the dark, and for once, you want something permanent, something that you can hold on to.

The world sees a picture-perfect smile but deep in those eyes are the remnants of the lost magic. You are neither sad nor happy, you just are tired of figuring out what you are supposed to do, and you are tired of just being.

Chapter 45

Sam didn't realize when he left Riya's place. He was walking around, lost in his thoughts. *Aarush! Best Friend! Mrs. Jennie's son!* It seemed the chapters of his life suddenly skipped a few pages and reached the end; a not so happy end! He felt he wasn't even a part of these chapters. It felt like the starting chapters from the next book that the author includes at the end of the book you are reading.

He couldn't wrap his head around how his life twisted in these past three days. Everything he had ever asked for was right there within his reach, and just when he thought he would grab it, it was all taken away.

My ladies? I know how to tame this fluttering butterfly!

Fucking know-how. No one knows my Riya better than I do.

He was feeling more insecure than ever.

Did he just lose her again?

Twelve years did make a difference! Why was he so confident that Riya was still in love with him? All these days when she was with him, she never said she loved him. The feelings might have been there, but of course, people change, and so does the emotions. She might be spending time with him as a long-lost friend.

She was a little jittery and resentful when they were at the restaurant. But the moment she came home and hugged

Aarush, her tensions somehow dissipated. She was back to the carefree girl in a second.

Is that how much Aarush affects her?

His thoughts turned to Aarush.

So, Aarush is Mrs. Jennie's son. But Riya told him they are just good friends. She is so close to Mrs. Jennie. Surely there must be something else going on too. Aarush seems to know a lot about Riya too. And she doesn't even mind him being so cocky.

Too hot to handle!

Then why was Mrs. Jennie giving me subtle hints all these days?

Maybe she wanted me to suffer. She knows how much Riya has gone through all these years. She cares for her and maybe wanted me to go through the same pain.

Maybe they are really just best friends.

I know, but she may have been sad and vulnerable. And Aarush has a kind of obvious charm to his ways.

Also, he is Mrs. Jennie's son.

Clear it up with Riya. There was indeed something going on between us all these days. The way she felt, I am sure, she meant it.

You may be a little too late. Did you forget your morning conversation? She surely was hinting that she doesn't believe in you anymore.

No. She is just a little lost. I know her! She needs to put her feet on the ground, and I am there to be her ground.

Then why are you so insecure?

I need to talk to her.

Sam was still worried about how the events turned. He was lost in the conversation that they were having at the restaurant before Mrs. Jennie called Riya. He knew Riya was right and that he had no right to expect her to forgive him and just resume from where they left.

Disoriented with his thoughts, Sameer decided to walk towards the boardwalk. He had never been so agitated in his life. All these years, he agonized over letting her go and not having the courage to stand up for their love. But he never thought how much she might have gone through. He knew that in a sane world, Riya shouldn't even bother to look at the guy who broke all his promises.

But you cannot deny the feelings we still share, Riya. They have only grown stronger.

He bought a crate of beer and sat in a corner facing the sea. He had never felt so broken. He gulped down the beers as if they would quench his thirst for a second chance with Riya. He knew he shouldn't be drinking much as it would cloud his rational mind. He wanted to drown his crippling feelings, the way he was drowning in his agony.

He had lost track of time while wandering around. The late afternoon sun was making him drowsy. Whenever he looked at it, he felt as if he was losing something. And today, of all the days, it was making Sameer dejected. Without thinking much, he dialed Riya's number, and to his surprise, Aarush picked up her phone.

"Riya?" Sam asked cautiously, trying hard to erase the scenarios cropping up in his head.

"Ms. Riya is a little busy cooking for me. I can pass on the message, though." Aarush said in a breezy manner.

"Aarush! Put it on the speaker." Sam heard Riya from the other side of the phone.

Speaker? She wants me to talk to her on loudspeaker in front of a third person. Is this the extent of bond that we share now?

Who says he is the third person? By the looks of it, you seem like a third person trying to invade their perfectly breezy life.

Sam was annoyed at the homely vibe they both emanated. He felt as if they were a well-settled couple baking on the weekend, and he was just a long-lost relative calling in to ask a favor. He disconnected the phone in frustration.

This was new territory.

Did he misinterpret her signals? Has she moved on? Was she spending time with him out of respect for all the time they had been together?

Sam was exhausted from the never-ending questions being bombarded in his head.

Maybe life isn't really that magnanimous. Perhaps you do get second chances but not the ones that have the power to change your life. Maybe meeting Riya was a way for life to mock him for letting a girl like her slip away so easily.

He didn't know what to do except occupying his mind with work. He was glad that he carried his bag with him. He opened his laptop and looked at the pile of work that had accumulated. Despite trying hard to immerse himself in work, he found it impossible to keep his thoughts off from whatever happened since the morning today. He couldn't fathom the uncertainty in Riya's voice. Even when they were just friends, Riya's eyes always held confidence and certainty when it came to their bond. But today, her eyes were skeptical and... *scared*, a little voice inside his head whispered.

He wanted to explain to Riya. He knew he was twelve years late, but he didn't want the lost time to define their bond.

The more he felt confident about his feelings, the more his mind drifted to the moments on her porch with Aarush. He had no idea what was going on between the two of them. But he desperately wanted to know. It was the kind of feeling students have when their results are declared. They get curious because they believed in their efforts but, at the same time, are scared too of the outcome.

He realized he had finished all his beer. He checked his phone for any message from Riya. Seeing the empty notification screen, he headed to buy more beer and some chips. He settled again with a beer in his hand and scrolled through their chats from these past few days. There was nothing special in those chats except the meeting times and places and regular niceties you share with acquaintances.

Was it all just a casual thing?

He tried hard to find hidden meanings in all the messages they had exchanged. A human mind is a strange machine. It fails to look at the things right in front of them and tries to find hidden meanings at useless places. Life is not always so complicated. You do not always need to be a monk and look for subtle signs. Sometimes it is right there, exactly how it should be.

He was feeling dizzy because of all the alcohol. As he saw a couple walk past him holding hands, he remembered how he had held Riya's hand while they were dancing during the last day of the workshop.

Come on, Riya! There was definitely something that you were also feeling.

As he lay there, he realized that the night had cooled the chaos down in his mind. Low on inhibitions and rational filters, he texted Riya.

"Hey. Can we meet for dinner?"

"Sorry. I am a little busy. Maybe tomorrow?"

Busy with what? Aren't you done cooking? Now, does he need you to feed him too?

Sam was surprised at his own thoughts. He was jealous of Aarush. Riya had explained it to him, but still, he couldn't grasp their friendship, especially when Riya has been behaving strangely. Had she been talking to him, he would have been sane.

He shook his head and typed his reply.

"No problem."

"You called in the afternoon too. What happened?"

At least she is replying. Yay!

"Nothing. Nothing. I wanted to ask you for dinner only. We left our conversation incomplete in the morning."

"Let's meet tomorrow?"

"Sure."

The chat seemed like walking on eggshells. Sam realized that he would have to wait for tomorrow to satisfy his thoughts.

Nights are the hardest when there is a restlessness creeping within you. At least during the day, the brightness filters through your mind and makes it all look like an illusion. But at night, there is no hiding behind the illusions of reality.

He gave up and started wandering aimlessly.

Chapter 46

Sam was walking along the boardwalk, and just as he turned around the corner, he happened to see Riya with her pretty hair flowing along with the breeze. Before he could savor the moment, he was disappointed to see Aarush sitting across her. Out of nowhere, he remembered Riya telling him that this was the best restaurant in Boothbay and that many people chose this place to propose.

Why the hell are they at such a posh restaurant?

Why do you think Sam? It has the perfect ambiance for a proposal. And obviously, Aarush knew Riya loves this place.

So this is where she was busy.

Despite his mind telling him otherwise, he decided to call her again. At times, the human mind cannot rationalize its own actions, especially when taken either out of love or insecurity.

"I am glad you have at least one friend who owns such a classy restaurant. Else we would never be able to afford food at this place." Riya laughed with Aarush.

"Having good friends is the only thing I am best at." Aarush said earnestly, raising the wine glass at Riya.

Riya shook her head and turned to look in her bag where her phone was ringing. *Sameer!* She turned the phone on silent and resumed her conversation with Aarush.

Aarush looked at her inquiringly.

"Sameer."

"The morning guy who wouldn't cross our house's threshold?" Aarush laughed mockingly at Sam's behavior in the morning.

"Aarush!"

"Why are you getting so worked up? And what does he want?" Aarush commented casually.

Riya rolled her eyes and let his questions dissipate in the aroma of food.

"Oh my God! Is this the bloke who forced you out of your own country?"

"Hey! It was my decision to come here for higher studies." Riya threw a piece of fries at Aarush, which he easily caught and ate, smiling at her.

"To escape him." Aarush said as a matter of fact. "It worked out well for me, though." Aarush said, enjoying the close bond they both share. "Hey, do you remember the time when I took you to that dance?" Aarush said, suddenly lighting up.

"And asked me to pretend to be your girlfriend. Yes, Aarush. I don't even know why I agreed. Poor girl!"

"What agreed? It was your once-in-a-lifetime chance to dance with someone so dashing. But no, not that! Remember you had so much to drink, and you slapped that girl when she came to confront me." Aarush was laughing uncontrollably.

"It was my first time having wine. I didn't know such small sips could be so hazardous. Did I say something to her?" Riya bent forward, really curious.

"You said, 'Don't you dare come even an inch closer to my man. Bitch! Don't fool around him. He is my fool, Hindi waala.'" Aarush said, mimicking Riya.

Riya placed her hands on her mouth in embarrassment. They both burst into laughter.

"My god! I still cannot believe I said those words."

"I told you, you are the best when you are drunk."

Riya punched him in his shoulder.

"But I would not want to be there when the hangover dissolves in your cells. You were wailing like an injured dog after we went home, and I tucked you in the bed. You were so loud that mom thought I pissed you off, like always, and threw me out. I had to walk back in that drunken state to my place to sleep. Such a pain you were!"

"Yeah, Mrs. Jennie grilled me the next day. She was sure it was you who caused a ruckus."

"Why does she love you so much? I am her original son."

"Who is not here most of the time. Unreliable jerk!" Riya pointed out to him.

"Hey, that's not fair. Sometimes you have to let your parents be."

Riya did her slow caps at his silly excuse and rolled her eyes.

"Hey. By the way, I had asked you for a favor. It has been months. I hope you haven't ruined it." Riya asked eagerly.

Aarush's eyes sparkled as he straightened himself. "What do I get when I hand it over to you?"

"I have done enough for you, you jerk!" Seeing that Aarush was unwavering, she gave up. "Fine. Whatever you want. Arghh! I hate you."

* * *

Sam was stunned to see how comfortably Riya was laughing with Aarush. He wanted to go nearer so that he could hear their conversation, but he satisfied himself with just watching those two. He suddenly realized how pathetic he was.

He was about to take a step back when he saw Aarush taking out some keys from his pocket.

"Tada..." Aarush threw the keys at Riya.

Sameer had never seen Riya so ecstatic about something. He heard her saying 'I love You' in her thrilled voice and hugged Aarush.

Sam stopped breathing.

So this is it. They may be moving in together.

He felt his cheeks getting wet. He was cemented to the ground. No matter how much he hated what was unfolding in front of him, he couldn't walk away. *Not again.* His heart had broken into pieces, and he was holding onto them with hope, which had no credibility in the given circumstances.

Sameer kept his eyes glued to the scene. He observed that Aarush was waiting for Riya to settle down before continuing.

"Now it's your turn to return the favor," Aarush said sincerely.

"Anything!" Riya was jubilant and couldn't stop looking at the keys.

"Riya." Aarush tried to bring her back to the table with all her senses.

"Yes, yes. So, what is it? And why the hell are you so nervous?"

At the corner, the scene unfolded slowly as ever in front of Sameer.

He saw Aarush taking a deep breath and placing a diamond ring in front of Riya.

Sam's eyes widened with shock. Before he knew, he was out and walking towards their table. He looked at Riya with anger that was bubbling with jealousy.

Chapter 47

"Sam! What are you…?"

Before she could complete her sentence, he pulled her hand, dropping the napkin from her lap, and kept walking towards the end of the boardwalk.

As they reached the end, she jerked her hand from his hold.

"Sam! What the hell do you think you are doing?"

He looked wounded as if this was a normal thing to do.

"What are you doing here? And what just happened?" She pointed towards the direction where she was just having her dinner with Aarush.

Sam was at a loss of words. He never thought Riya could be mad at him. Maybe he was really mistaken in understanding her. *Twelve years did make a difference, after all.*

"Sameer! I am asking you something." Riya shook him out of his thoughts.

"Why did you raise my hopes if you didn't plan on being with me?" Before Sam knew, the words were out of his mouth, served right there on a platter without dressing.

"What? What the hell do you mean?" Riya was appalled at what Sam was saying.

"Didn't he just propose to you? And looking at you, it seemed you were elated." Sam sneered. He was here to apologize to Riya, but the scene that unfolded in front of him transformed his emotions.

Riya folded her hands and looked at him with utter disdain. She couldn't believe what Sam was thinking.

"You don't know what you are talking about. Let me go. He is waiting for…" She turned around to leave when he grabbed her hand and pulled her towards himself. He held both her hands and made her face him.

"Look at me!" Sam held her hand tightly and jerked her.

"What do you want?" Suddenly Riya's anger spiked.

"Look, Riya!"

Riya pulled herself from his hold and pointed at him.

"No! You look Sameer! You were the one who married! You were the one who left! You were the one who denied every feeling that we shared! Now you just can't barge in. Let me live my life!"

"Riya. Give me a chance, at least." All his anger dissipated in an instant.

"What is your problem?"

"You!" He waved his hand towards her as if it was a magic wand that would make her understand what he wanted to say.

"Excuse me!"

He lowered his voice, almost velvety.

"You are my problem. Why don't you ever understand expressions or my eyes or… argh… !!!! I am madly in love with you. I cannot for a second stop thinking about the time we have spent together. Every single thing reminds me of you. I know I was foolish when I let you go before. It was one of the biggest mistakes of my life. No matter how much I want, I cannot change the past, or the choices I made. I regret these twelve years every second, Riya. But we got our second chance, and I don't want to ruin it. We are perfect for each other. You make me want to live. You make me want to love you. I want to make up for all the tears you have shed. I want to hold you close and make your heart beat and make up for all those times you felt numb, Riya. I want to make you smile in a way that you forget what it is to even feel sad. I want to love you, Riya. I want to fill your life with all the happy emotions. I love you."

"Wh…" *oh my god! I will faint. Is this really happening?* She tried hard to control the emotions that were running berserk. Sameer never had, in all those years, expressed his feelings so fervently. Her insides were melting, and she knew she wouldn't be able to hold it in any longer. Every question that had been nagging her all these days was being answered. Every skepticism was being repudiated with the truth.

"You are driving me insane. How can you not feel it? How can you be so casual? I know you care! I know you were there with me all these past days. I know you felt it too." Sam takes a breath and holds her gaze, "Don't look at me like that, Riya. Your face is as talkative as your stupid mouth. And yes, I felt it too. And here you are, having dinner with him just because you are mad at me."

"Sam…"

He cut her off and pulled her closer from her waist, and lifted her chin towards his eyes.

"Look, I know I missed being with you for twelve years. I know I was a fool for letting you go. But here we are. Please don't take this chance away from us. I can keep you happier than him. I know he is more charming than I am, but Riya, you know how much I love you. You know you make my heart beat. I want to spend all my nights sleeping with no one but you. I want to sleep in your arms and wake up to your face every single day of my life. And I know you want it too." He looked deep into her eyes before continuing, "At least the Riya I know, she wanted it all too. I love you, Riya."

He looked at her and took a step towards her, held her face with both hands, and took in her lips. His hands moved in her hair, pulling her closer to savor her lips. Riya surrendered herself to his hold. She could feel in her heart the sanctity of the words that Sameer just spoke. Her hand moved to his hair as her lips got lost in his passion.

As they parted, Sameer turned to see Aarush standing across them, with his hands in his pocket, looking amused.

"Aarush," Riya whispered.

Chapter 48

Lake Palace, Udaipur, India
July 2012

Riya was at her cousin Suhana's wedding. It was the sangeet ceremony where both the bride and groom's family danced in celebration. But more often than not, it turned out to be a competition between the two sides. They had been planning for this event since the day Suhana's parents agreed to her marriage to Arjun. They had gone over the program and the list of dances a thousand times, just to make sure there was no repetition of songs.

Finally, it was their turn to show off to the groom's side how well prepared they were.

Wait till we go on the stage.

She had already told everyone to hoot and cheer when they head towards the stage. And as expected, her cousins and relatives were whistling and cheering incessantly.

Good. That sets the pace. Let's roll and show them who's the boss!

Just as she was about to take the position, she felt she saw someone looking at her. She felt someone move around the groom's friends. She shook away the thought. She had been preparing for this dance for fifteen days now. It was challenging to coordinate with all the cousins, knowing they all lived in different cities. It was hardly two days back when they all were finally in one place and practiced together.

When it came to dancing, she knew she was arrogant.

As they took their positions, the song boomed from the speaker. She was lost in the dance. She never felt happier than when she was dancing. All the cheering reverberated in her ears, and she just went with the flow; the hook steps, the jumping, the teasing. The crowd was ecstatic. She could see everyone smiling and cheering for them. They ended their dance with a bang. The poppers burst open, and the entire stage was filled with ribbons.

This was her drug of choice! Dancing and the applause that follows.

And just while she was basking in all the cheering, the song changed. Everyone stopped as the cousins looked around. She pointed to the event guy asking what's wrong. The guy gestured to someone behind the decorations. She tried to see who the hell dared to intrude in their performance.

And just then, the speakers exploded the song "Hawa Hawa" from the movie Rockstar.

And the limelight stealer came into view, looking at Riya with deep, challenging eyes.

How dare…

Wait! What the hell! Why is he looking at me like that?

She raised her eyes, conveying that he could have waited for them to get down before climbing on the stage for his cannot-wait-awesome performance. Before she could take a step towards the edge of the stage, he pulled her towards him with such passion and twirled her that she couldn't realize what happened.

What the…?

She looked at him with wide eyes. She was about to snap at his stupidity, especially in front of so many people, but he had an earnest expression on his face. He twirled her back to the other side and bowed to her slightly. Just so slightly that she knew it was meant for her to acknowledge.

Does he want me to dance with him?

Before she could answer her own question, the volume increased. *"Hawa Hawa .... naachi re magan."* The way he looked at her, she knew she couldn't resist. Moreover, this song always made her want to dance. And just like that, they were dancing, as if they had been dancing together since forever. He was spectacular with his arms and feet. They understood each other's movements and expressions. He rolled her towards him and swung her in his arms, and she leaned in with a soft gasp.

"Chidh kar gusse me bola raja..." He moved towards her siblings and enacted with them. Everybody had started cheering. This guy brought fun to the dance and was dancing amongst her cousins to the beats of this song.

She was feeling completely out of herself that she bared herself to the song.

He dances so damn well!

She shed her layers of sophistication and went around in a circle, imagining her cousins as the wall, *"sone ki deeware... mujhe khushi na ye de paae..."*

He started laughing in appreciation while blushing a little. He was enjoying how dramatic she made the steps. She couldn't help but laugh with him. She came close to him and knelt down on her knees *"azaadi de de mujhe... mere khuda... le le tu daulat aur kar de riha..."*

He was hysterical now, and so was everyone. She had never seen such a magnificent impromptu performance where everybody was involved. Nor had she ever had so much fun, especially with someone who somehow took away her limelight.

Everyone was cheering wholeheartedly. It was such maddening chaos saturated with jubilance and laughter. As the song ended, he brought everyone together, held their hands, and bowed.

Just as she was about to step down the stage, he offered his hand and helped her.

Huhh!!! Gentleman?

"Hey!" He looked at her.

Speak! He is waiting for you to say something.

She had no idea what to say.

Did she just forget how to complete a sentence? Before she could make up another line, he spoke.

"Coffee?"

Wow! This guy is something. He just ruined my performance, and now he is asking me out.

Yeah, Riya. In your dreams! He is just being nice. Moreover, his performance was better than yours.

"I don't think they have coffee here. There are pretty great Mojitos, though." Riya tried to joke casually.

Was that a joke? Why do you even bother to joke? You are bad at jokes!

"I gotta run now. Arjun will kill me."

See! That's what you do to people when you try to joke.

He started turning but stopped. "I was asking for coffee after the wedding, by the way."

Oh!

"Are you still here?" He shook her from her internal monologue. She realized that she hadn't uttered a word yet.

"Oh ya ya. Sorry. Umm… how do you even know Arjun?"

Her voice sounded skeptical, which offended him. But suddenly, his expressions changed, and he was grinning at her.

"Do you think I am freeloading in a wedding?"

"Umm…" Riya looked around as if caught in the act of judging someone.

"Wow! You actually think so? Seriously? Well, I have an official invitation as the ex-roommate of the groom. Actually to-be-ex in two days." When Riya didn't answer, he continued, "You are looking as if you still don't believe me. Do you?" He asked, folding his arms. Riya noticed the bulge of his biceps, causing creases to the kurta he was wearing. She focussed her head and continued her skepticism.

"If you are so close to him, why haven't I seen you since yesterday? All his friends have been loitering around."

"I came this morning only, and since then, I have been busy with Arjun. That jerk didn't know his dance steps and was so nervous dancing with Suhana. He has been pissing me off so much since morning. Even a kid learns faster than that psycho." The comfort that he radiated was so natural that Riya forgot that she just met him.

She laughed and remembered how funny Arjun dances. She had made fun of him with her cousins.

"So you taught him the solo he did?" She tried to say without showing him any hint of laughter but failing badly.

"Hey, don't look at me. A guy can only teach so much. He has to move the legs at the end. I can't do it for him."

She laughed again.

Why am I laughing so much?

"So, coffee tomorrow?"

"I can't. I have my flight. I am leaving just after the ceremonies."

"So, you want an expensive coffee?" He raised his eyebrows.

There's the grin again. What is wrong with his lips? Why does he grin so much?

"What? No! I mean…Wait. What do you mean?"

"Relax! I am also headed to the airport. Arjun told me to coordinate with Suhana's cousin, who is leaving by Air India flight. I suppose you are her?"

"Yeah. I am her."

She had started enjoying the conversation and, moreover, his company. Just then, his phone rang. And she could hear someone yelling on the other side.

He waved the phone at her and started running towards the stage.

"See you tomorrow."

* * *

The next morning after saying goodbye to everyone, literally, everyone, Riya got in the car and rested her head against the seat. She was exhausted from all the dancing from the night before.

"Aahh! Take me home!" She said aloud.

"You are not really my kind. But that's okay. I don't mind."

"Excuse me!" Riya turned around to see the same guy who danced with her yesterday, reading a brochure and grinning.

"Aarush, by the way." He introduced himself, realizing that they didn't exchange their names after the dance yesterday.

"Riya." She suddenly turned towards him, "Hey! Wait! Were you here before I climbed in?"

"Pretty much." Aarush closed the brochure and packed it in his bag.

"Oh!"

"You were probably too exhausted from so many hugs you wanted to exchange that you didn't notice." He said, waving everyone goodbye.

"Why does it sound sarcastic?"

"Maybe because it is," Aarush said as a matter of fact.

"What do you mean? What's so wrong in wanting to hug everyone you love?"

"Exactly my point."

"I cannot see any. Not that I even want to, anyway." Riya rolled her eyes and rested her head on the seat.

"Okay. Suit yourself. Not that you like to face the truth anyway." Aarush was having fun toying with this hyper-animated girl.

"You do not even know me! And what is that smug for?" Riya's voice turned into a shrill.

"Well, you seemed to love hugging everyone. And looking at the scene, you didn't really want to go anywhere but here. And now you are dying to go back home. Either that was fake, or this is."

"Hey, that's being too judgmental. I do love my family. And I won't be visiting them at all anytime soon. So, I was just taking my time. But it tires me out. I would rather pack my bags and leave early in the morning without meeting anyone."

"You could have not knocked on every door for a goodbye hug."

"Where the hell have you been?" Riya looked at him skeptically.

"Right here," Aarush said, smiling satisfactorily.

"Whatever. They would have felt bad had I left just like that."

"See, just now, you said you wanted to take your time because you won't be seeing them anytime soon. Now you are putting it on them that they would feel bad. From where I was seeing, you were enjoying waking everyone up and saying goodbye. Then you claim it tires you out, and you would rather go unannounced. I don't understand girls!"

Aarush shook her head in slight mockery. He suddenly turned to Riya, "Maybe you were scared that despite all the dances and fun you did, they wouldn't miss you once you are gone?"

"Are you even making sense?" Riya, taken aback by such arrogance and tried to shake it off. She knew he was getting on her nerves.

"Well, that's what I think. That's why you were angry yesterday when I stole the show."

"I wasn't angry. I wouldn't be talking to you after the dance had I been angry." She looked at him knowing he wasn't convinced. She continued, "Okay, maybe a little bit. But that was because I had been preparing for that dance for quite some time. Obviously, a person needs acknowledgment for the efforts. And it was all going as I had imagined until you came with your arrogance and moves. And now prattling early in the morning as if you know me from ages and judging me."

Riya stopped midway when she realized that she was just blabbering, and Aarush was looking at her intently.

"Sorry! My mind is too tired to filter."

"That works well for me." Aarush grinned at her.

"Excuse me?" *This guy is too much! Why am I even entertaining him?*

"So, coffee today? I hope you haven't changed your mind?"

"Do I even have the option?" Her anger and frustration had surprisingly receded.

"No, you don't."

Damn the attitude again!

"So anyway, why are you headed to the US?" Riya tried to shift to regular topics of conversation between strangers.

"I am not."

"You are not?"

"No. I am going to Cambodia."

"You said we are going on the same flight." Riya was suddenly confused.

"Did I?" He smiled. "My flight is not until late afternoon. But I thought it's better to go together than have someone send a car for me again later."

When Riya didn't reply, he continued, "What did you think?" Aarush raised his eyebrows at Riya.

Riya had no idea why she was a little disappointed. Aarush seemed like a lovely friend, especially when he took care of Arjun the whole night yesterday. Though he was a bit arrogant and irritating, it would have been nice to have someone to talk to on the flight. She had occupied her mind with the wedding and the dance but knew that the moment her mind rested, she would fall back into the abyss.

"Nothing!"

"You know your face gives you away. The more you try to hide something, the more it opens wide."

Damn! Is he flirting with me?

And why does he make such remarks? We have hardly talked for more than 10 minutes since yesterday.

"So, why?" Riya tried to shift the focus from her insides out to his.

"Work!"

This was known territory. Riya learned that talking about a guy's work keeps him at bay and keeps the focus off of you. Usually, men don't shy away from talking about what they do and, more often than not, are entirely occupied in boasting in front of the girl that they completely forget asking about the girl. And Riya was in no mood to be under the microscope, especially by this guy who surprisingly could read her so well.

"I see. What do you do?" Riya probed.

"As of now? Nothing!"

The look on her face made him laugh. "I want to open a dance travel group, and for that, I am having a meeting with a couple of investors."

"Dance travel group? Like dancers who travel?" Riya was surprised at such a kind of work, but it piqued her interest.

"Not just that. In my mind, we would be a group of dancers who would travel to culturally rich places all over the world. Learn the dance forms, and then move in the interior parts of the country and teach those dance forms to the underprivileged people, who often dreamt of dancing but couldn't because of obvious reasons."

Riya was listening with awe. It is very rare that a man not only is following his passion but is also working towards making other people follow theirs.

"Did I just impress you?" Aarush said in a confident tone, happy with himself.

"As much as I hate to admit, you did!" Riya had a renewed sense of respect for Aarush.

"Nice! What about you? What's there in store for you in The States?"

"I am an architect." Riya didn't elaborate on why she had chosen to go to The States when her entire family was in India. She wished he won't ask her the reason for doing a degree like Architecture from anywhere but India. She was in no mood to expose her barren life to a stranger who was charming enough to make her vulnerable.

"A dancer architect. Hey, you could design our camper."

Riya looked at him, not believing the kind of idea this guy has.

"Why don't you join me?" Aarush asked earnestly.

Damn, he is charming.

"Travel with you?"

"And a couple of other dancers. You enjoy dancing. And you could also help us with our campervan. I can handle the technical stuff, but the design bowls me over."

"Surprisingly, that's one of my dreams. Not the dancing part, but traveling in a camper van and exploring different cultures."

Riya was surprised at how easily she told such an intimate detail to someone she just met.

"See! Maybe we met so that we can fulfill each other's dreams." Aarush said nonchalantly.

Riya was touched by his words. She had no idea why, but she always felt this strange connection with people who talked about fulfilling dreams. But she knew she had a lot of things to deal with before pursuing her dream. She had to first manage the chaos in her soul. Just then, she heard the announcement that her flight was ready to board.

"That's me! Good luck with your project."

"It was a pleasure, Riya." Aarush held her hand and pressed it warmly.

Chapter 49

"That is it?" Sameer said, unable to believe what he just heard from Aarush and Riya.

"That was it!" Riya said, folding her hands.

"But look at my bad luck. She followed me here." Aarush nudged at Riya.

Riya glared at Aarush. *He somehow hasn't developed the art of understanding the situation and how to joke or when,* Riya thought to herself.

"It wasn't till I saw him again at Mrs. Jennie, after a year, that we became friends." Riya cleared the confusion, if any, in Sameer's mind.

"And I realized how totally crazy she is. The girl I met at the wedding was a sane version of this girl living next to my mom. Can you believe she chops off her hair if she is way too bored or sometimes when she is frustrated? Anyway, I was going through a rough phase at that time, and your girl helped me like a knight in shining armor. She is a hell of an expert when it comes to relationship advice. Well for other's relationships." He winked at her.

"Well, it's easier when it doesn't concern yourself," Riya said, as a matter of fact, looking at Sameer.

Sameer didn't know what to say. He was still trying to grasp the story they told about how they met.

"And the keys?" Sameer asked slowly, wanting to know the truth but afraid of what it might be.

"Those are the keys to my campervan. I had asked him to handle the technical stuff since he has been driving one for his travels."

Campervan!

"By the way, that was a hell of a kiss." Aarush grinned at Sam. "But dude, you could have waited for our dinner to get over."

Sam, still bubbling with insecurity, held Riya's hand as if to mark his territory.

Riya giggled. Sam looked at her with questioning eyes.

"Does he not believe me because I am bloody charming, and he feels anyone can fall for me, or is he just possessive?" Aarush said, pointing at Sameer.

Riya looked at Aarush, pointed at the ring he was holding, and said solemnly, "He saw the ring."

Aarush instantly understood what just happened. Looking at Sam's expressions, how angry he was, he couldn't control himself. He held the ring and asked Riya, "You still need to return my favor. So what do you think?"

Riya tried to contain her laughter, knowing well enough that Aarush was just toying with Sameer now. Sameer exploded with anger thinking how brazen Aarush is to ask her out despite him standing right there. He charged towards Aarush when a bewildered Riya stopped him.

Both Aarush and Riya start laughing hysterically, leaving Sameer at a loss of words.

"Dude! I am proposing to my long-time girlfriend. I just wanted to show it to Riya and ask her for some advice. You know, from a woman to man."

"But isn't this place too fancy for asking just advice? You could have asked at home too." Sameer wasn't ready to let go of his insecurity.

"Sameer!" Riya was feeling embarrassed.

"Sorry, bro, I'll ask my friend to buy a small cafe next time rather than such a fancy place, as it causes a stirring of emotions in envious lovers."

"Oh!" Sam was at a loss of words. *So this was Aarush's friend's place, and that's why they were here.* Sam had never been so flustered in his life. He misunderstood everything. Jealousy and insecurity overtook his rationality.

"I am sorry. I…"

"Relax, dude. Now shall we go have dinner?"

Sam hesitated.

"Don't worry, you do not have to propose to eat there." Aarush lightened the mood and strode towards the restaurant.

Chapter 50

"I never knew you could ever be so insecure or jealous," Riya said as they were finishing their dessert. Aarush had left early, saying he had a couple of preparations to take care of before proposing the next day.

"How can I not be? We were madly in love with each other, then I got married to someone else and was gone for twelve years. Now when I meet you again, I have a daughter and have grown old. But you haven't aged at all. If possible, you have become more charming that it aches to not be able to hold you every time I see you. How can I not be insecure? I am a walking advertisement that says don't fall for this guy. He is not only unreliable but also comes with baggage, and Aarush is the kind of guy that any woman can fall in love with."

Sameer was suddenly chatty and impatient. He wanted to fill in the gap of all these years by talking and expressing as much as possible. He had almost lost Riya.

"Wow! You have lost faith in your charm, it seems." Riya teased him, "I thought no matter what happened, you can entice any girl with your charming smile. You have become real."

"I can still charm any girl with my smile, but as for you, you know what lies beneath it. It's redundant when it comes to you. With you, all I have got is *real*."

"You have grown so much in an hour."

Riya chuckled as Sam blushed and became more embarrassed.

"And moreover, ever since you went without saying anything to me that day, it has been driving me mad. I have racked my brains thinking about what you read and the decisions that you might have made. It scared the shit out of me. I thought I lost you again."

The mention of letters turned her silent. Sam instantly knew her behavior had something to do with those letters.

He didn't know how to ask her for the fear of finding something that would tear them apart. The silence was filled with the scratch and turn of fork and spoon.

"Sameer."

"Riya."

They both said at the same time.

"Go ahead." Riya said.

Sameer was a little nervous, and he had no idea why he was so agitated. *I need to take this chance*, he thought to himself.

"Umm… Did you… read all the letters?"

Riya nodded, letting Sameer take the moment ahead. Till now, both of them had behaved as if they were okay with the way things were, and the years they spent apart were nothing but pleasant. They made each other believe that life had been good to them. But now, both of them knew how vulnerable they always were.

"All of them?"

Riya simply nodded. She had rarely seen Sameer so nervous. They paid for their dinner and were walking towards his home.

"Is that why you didn't want to talk to me?"

"I don't know Sameer. Reading those letters brought back all the twelve years I spent trying to fight away every urge to contact you. I couldn't believe myself when I felt a pang of jealousy while reading that there were girls who were doting on you. I was scared to feel all those things. I didn't even know what you felt."

"Riya."

"Sameer, no matter how strong I was, it took my entire strength to accept the reality. And I didn't want to be in that situation again. Reading those letters made me realize what you also went through, and it broke my heart. I may have started wanting you again, but I was scared of reality. And then I saw my handwriting, which took me back to the time when I cried myself to sleep every night, not sure of where my love lacked that you didn't choose me. I was scared of your absence again."

"Why didn't you say anything then? Why did you run away?" He had tried to understand her reaction in every possible way and was bowled over.

"I didn't know where we stood. I didn't want to risk anything again without being sure. It took me a long time to gather the pieces you broke me into. I didn't even know I had millions of pieces scattered around."

"Riya. I cannot believe how silly you are. I am glad I did what I did today. You still haven't learned to rightfully ask for what is yours, and always has been."

They realized they had reached his home. He opened the door and let Riya enter.

"Are you still talking to the dumb office girls?"

"What?" Sam was shocked. He couldn't believe what she just said. He thought she would question him about what he told Anaya and about his feelings.

He didn't understand what just happened.

"Show me your blocked list," Riya said, holding her hand out.

Sam knew he had just lost to her charm, yet again. He laughed with tears in his eyes, and the evening became more beautiful. He hugged her tightly, savoring in her fragrance that had always made him go crazy.

Unable to control himself anymore, he cupped her face in his hands, and kissed her passionately. Noticing that Riya neither stopped him nor took a step back, he pulled her from her waist and tilted her face, making her face him. He looked into her eyes with burning passion and kissed her lips deeply.

They could feel each other's hearts as years of longing surfaced.

Riya brought her hands around his neck and pulled him closer. Her hands grazed through his hair as they explored their tongues with the passion they didn't know was hidden beneath the life they had been living.

"You are blushing like it was your first kiss." He tried to ease off the atmosphere.

"It felt like that." She said, biting her lips consciously.

"I feel like that every time I kiss you."

He held her face and rubbed his thumb over her cheeks. "I have missed you terribly."

Riya smiled as he kissed her knuckles and then her forehead.

"I have missed you too."

"I am sorry, Riya. I am sorry for all those nights when you must have cried to sleep. I am sorry for shaking your faith in love; for every moment when you might have questioned your love for us. I am sorry. I really am. And I know, no amount of apology will be enough to make up for the pain you have gone through. But I will spend my entire lifetime to make it up to you. I am really sorry, Riya."

They hugged and took in the moment.

Chapter 51

"How have you been?" Sameer asked, holding her hand.

They had moved to his backyard with wine. Their inhibitions tonight were lower than before, and they felt more comfortable with each other. Sam had covered Riya with a blanket, and they were lying together looking at the stars. They both knew now what they felt for each other. The wall between them, though transparent, was nowhere now. They had acknowledged that life did happen to them, yet here they were, ready to live it all over again.

Riya looked at Sam inquiringly.

"I know we have frequently been meeting each other lately. I know what's going on with you, more or less. But I want to know how you have been? All these years? Were you happy? Where were you? Was it so easy to disappear? I looked for you everywhere." Sameer asked with a hint of pain in his voice.

Riya, palpable to his pain, kissed his hand and tried to smile.

"No, Sameer. It wasn't easy. It wasn't easy at all. It was one hell of a time. I thought I would lose myself. The day you got married was the day I knew it was time for me to fulfill my promise of letting you go. I wanted you to be happy. I truly did. But I hated the fact that you were happy with someone else. I blamed you so many times for letting me go. I kept my promise of letting you go when the time came, but you broke yours by letting me go. It shattered me. I was afraid I would never be able to feel again."

Sameer wiped tears from her eyes, unaware that he was crying too.

"I am sorry, Riya. Is that why you were scared these past three days? That I will let you go again?"

Riya nodded slowly. Looking at how Riya was feeling, he pulled her close.

"Why didn't you ever try to contact me all these years? Text, WhatsApp, e-mail, letter? You literally disappeared."

"I was scared. I was scared of loving you too much. I was scared that I'll ruin it for you. I was often just a click away from sending you an e-mail or a second away from dropping off the letters. Maybe I loved you way too much to express my love like that. And I thought maybe you do not need me anymore."

"Need you anymore? Riya, you were the breath I took." Sameer looked deep in her eyes as he released her from his embrace, "I am sorry for letting you down. I spent countless nights thinking about us, and the regrets kept mounting. I tried so much to find you everywhere. Twelve years Riya! Twelve years! We lost twelve years to life!"

"I used to pass by your place every now and then when I was in Ahmedabad, trying to look for signs of your happiness. I wanted to make my heart understand that it made the right decision. Then one day, I saw you playing with a little child."

"Anaya," Sameer whispered.

Riya nodded.

"You looked so happy and content. And it was my cue to let you be. That day I decided that I need to live my life. I felt that my love for you deserved at least this respect of being strong enough to let my happiness float. And that was the day I applied for a course here, and soon I moved."

"You never fell in love again?"

"I never fell out of love, Sameer. How would I have fallen in love again?"

Sam looked at her. Every moment they had spent together twelve years back was playing live in front of him. He felt that God had blessed him with a second life to choose to live it with the person who mattered the most to him.

"How did I let you go!" Sameer whispered.

Riya moved her hands in his hair and embraced the silence of these past years. Sameer held her hand and placed it on his heart, which was beating wildly. They both looked at each other with years of recognition.

"Can you give me another chance to be the reason for your smiles? I know I don't deserve any, and there is absolutely no reason for you to trust me. But… can you?"

Riya smiled at him and kissed his forehead.

Sameer instantly sat and looked at her.

"Sure? I won't let you go anywhere this time. Time has made me too possessive."

"That I have seen."

Sam chuckled and hugged her close to him. They had spent enough time apart that now he didn't want even a second to be away from her. He had missed her fragrance. He had missed how her hair smelled when she rested her head on his shoulder. He had missed how perfectly she snuggled in his arms.

He had missed the feeling of her smile on his neck when she hugged him.

* * *

"Sameer," Riya said cautiously while having their morning coffee.

"We will tell Anaya when she visits next." Sam, understanding what Riya was about to say, cuts her off.

"How did you know I…"

He came close and kissed her forehead.

"You are an extension of my own soul Riya. Don't worry. Anaya likes you a lot. And you know from the letters how much she wanted me to meet you." He said while switching on some music.

"But…"

"Riya. I found you after twelve years. Let's not spoil this morning by thinking of anything other than us. I know Anaya. She loves you. Don't you think I have thought about all this already?"

Sam looked at Riya and increased the volume of the song, and came towards her.

"*Wo subah toh bewajah ho..*

Ki gujre bina tumhare jiski raat.."

He held her close and tucked her hair, and looked her in the eyes.

"I don't want to spend any more such mornings where you aren't with me the night before. You were here with me last night, and that makes this morning nothing like all those that I spent waking these past twelve years." He held her hands and looked deep into her eyes. "Riya, let us promise to love each other; forever! Your kind of *forever!*"

Chapter 52

The days that followed were as sweet as honey. Riya didn't stop being sarcastic every now and then about how Sameer behaved when Aarush showed her the ring, and Sameer battled them all for Riya's smile. He knew they had a long way ahead of them. They were taking one year at a time.

They wanted to immerse themselves in their dream world. Aarush kept invading their lunches every now and then, which made them stay in touch with reality. Sameer was still not happy with the prospect of having such a charming guy around Riya. He knew his insecurity was baseless, but he wanted her all to himself.

But there was always one thought that nagged both of them. Anaya! Sameer didn't want to talk to Anaya about him and Riya on the phone. Deep in his heart, he knew Anaya would be thrilled to hear about them since she adored Riya, but he wanted Anaya to really want to be with Riya.

Loving someone as a kind person and loving someone as your family are two totally different things. He knew Anaya had initially struggled while he was divorcing. He did not want Anaya to go through any insecure feelings regarding his own life choices. Despite everything, he had faith in Anaya and his bond, and it kept him confident.

"Riya, I will be going to Portland tomorrow to meet Anaya," Sameer called Riya one afternoon.

"Oh. I hope everything is fine." Riya was genuinely concerned as she knew that parents generally were not allowed to visit boarding school during weekdays.

"Yes, yes. She skipped her classes to play cricket, the third time in a week." Sameer rolled his eyes.

Riya laughed at him. They discussed a long time ago how studies and sports should be balanced in schools rather than having an hour of sports on Saturdays or twice a week. She knew Sameer would love for Anaya to grow into a sportsman.

"Do you want to come?" Sameer asked. He had thought that taking Riya to meet Anaya could prove to be a buffer and make Anaya realize that they are really close. He was running out of options on ways to talk to Anaya about their relationship.

"I would love to. But I am resuming my work from tomorrow. In fact, I just came to the school to collect the details for the upcoming semester. When do you have to leave? I'll be free by 2."

"Sharp 11:30 am." Riya laughed as Sameer mimicked the principal. She had just had a glimpse of her when they had dropped Anaya last time. *We have come a long way since then,* Riya thought to herself.

"Oh! Good luck with the complaints then."

"Not really. I have been summoned there a lot of times. I think the principal and I have our side of speeches prepared by now."

"You don't need anyone else to spoil your kid, Sameer. You are more than enough."

"Of course! Anyway, can we prepone our dinner today and have it a little early, if it is okay with Mrs. Jennie?"

"Yes. Sure. By the way, Mrs. Jennie cannot wait to meet you again. I wonder what you two talked about when you came over that day."

"That's our secret. Shit! My eggs!" Riya heard some chaos on the other side, "Okay, I gotta go… see you soon."

She kept the phone in her bag and wrapped up her work. She headed home. On the way, she picked up some wine for the night. As she reached home, Riya thought of sending something to Anaya. She looked around her stuff and found a scarf that she had painted. She wrapped it up in paper and wrote a simple note.

Because pretty girls always wear pretty scarves.

As the night descended, Mrs. Jennie's home was filled with different kinds of aromas.

"My darling, you have a radiant aura around you." Mrs. Jennie said, kissing Riya's forehead as she stepped in ready for the evening.

"Radiant aura! Is she a divine lady or what?" Aarush chuckled as he set the table outside.

"Mr. Jealous!" Riya smirked at him.

"You have your personal Mr. Jealous, Reese. I am nothing compared to him." Aarush teased her as she brought the dishes outside.

"Don't you two fight again." Mrs. Jennie looked at the gate and saw Sameer. "Hi, Darling. Come on in."

"We were just talking about you." Aarush chuckled as Riya hit him.

Sameer couldn't help but still feel a bit uncomfortable around Aarush. He walked towards Mrs. Jennie and kissed her on her cheeks. Riya kept the dishes on the table and hugged Sameer. He inhaled her fragrance and wished they were alone.

They sat down for dinner and absorbed the crisp evening.

"Sameer, Riya tells me you are going to meet Anaya tomorrow?" Mrs. Jennie asked, handling a bowl of pasta to him.

Sameer nodded as he took a spoonful of pasta in his plate.

"Does she know about you two?"

"Not yet. I don't want to tell her on the phone. I am waiting for her to come home so that I can talk to her properly."

"You are scared of your daughter's reaction." Mrs. Jennie laughed.

"Believe me, Mrs. Jennie. I am freaking out. I know she loves Riya. But I want her to love her as family, you know." Sameer held Riya's hand and smiled at her.

"She is a smart girl. More mature than you two, at least more mature than Aarush here."

"Hey!" Aarush exclaimed.

"Her maturity is what terrifies me. I am afraid she would go along with it just because it makes me happy." Sameer spoke sincerely, remembering his daughter.

"She will understand. Have faith in her." Mrs. Jennie patted his hands.

Sameer nodded in acknowledgment.

"I am glad you guys realized your feelings. It would have hurt to see two people, so much in love, give up easily."

"Thanks to the key and the ring." Aarush winked at Riya, who returned the look with a glare.

"You know, Sameer, the day I first saw Riya stepping out of the car and unloading her luggage, I was in awe. She had so little. I have seen girls traveling with so much luggage. But here was this girl, who was shifting her entire life in just two boxes. One of which was marked 'books and journals.'"

"I was starting a new life," Riya said, looking somewhere far away.

"I found a daughter in her. Aarush was always so independent that I never got to protect him like a mother. He was always bossing me around. He rarely needed my protection. Riya made me feel like a mother. She was like a tiny flower, trying to bloom in harsh weather."

Sameer was listening to Mrs. Jennie intently. He wanted to meet the Riya who had come here and embraced this new life. He smiled at her affectionately.

"You guys are depressing me. Reese, why don't I tell him of your lesser-known facts when you were not a flower but a thorn." Aarush raised his eyebrows and laughed as Riya glared at him.

They talked about little things as the night matured. Riya smiled at the moment they were sharing. It was everything that she had wanted to feel all these years.

They finished the dinner and cleaned. Riya went inside her home and brought a gift-wrapped packet, and handed it to Sameer.

"For Anaya."

Sameer smiled affectionately and kissed her on her forehead.

Chapter 53

"Hey, my master blaster."

"Papa!" Anaya runs and hugs Sameer. He ruffled her hair and kissed her forehead.

"How's the weather inside?" Sameer asked, pointing at the principal's office. Anaya shrugged, and they walked inside the principal's office.

After almost 30 minutes of serious discussion, Sameer and Anaya came out of the office and relaxed. They were surprised when the principal allowed Sameer to take Anaya home for the weekend.

"Hey buddy, look, I am all for your sports or anything that you want to do, but do not break the rules," Anaya looked at Sam skeptically, "too frequently."

"You have promised me this time not to skip classes anymore. And promises…"

Anaya cut him off and said in an ominous voice. "And promises are meant to be sacred."

"That's my girl!" Beamed Sameer.

Anaya laughed at Sameer, and they walked towards the car. She exclaimed as she saw the wrapped bright yellow gift.

"Oh, I forgot. Ms. Riya sent it for you."

"Oh wow!" She opened the packet excitedly and was thrilled to see a new hand-painted scarf. She took it out and tied it around her neck.

"She is so awesome!" Anaya twirled around excitedly.

Her eyes suddenly moved to the note Riya had written, and somehow, the handwriting captured her attention. She couldn't relate where she had seen that handwriting, but she felt some kind of attachment to that handwriting. She couldn't quite place the feeling.

"Can we go meet her when we reach? I want to thank her."

"Sure, my love, if she is free from her work," Sameer said as she fixed her scarf correctly.

"She always takes out time for us," Anaya said in adoration.

Sameer smiled at her and moved his hands over her hair. She dozed off for a while, while Sam took some office calls.

On the way, they stopped for lunch.

"So now tell me, why did you skip your classes?"

Anaya looked at Sameer guiltily.

"I had missed a few sessions of training, and I had to cover up. So I skipped. And anyway, it was History. It's useless, papa."

History. Is it really useless? Can you keep aside the history with someone and start afresh? But isn't it History that bonds you strongly?

Sameer felt his mind drifting to Riya and how things turned out for them.

Had it not been for the history that they shared with each other, they wouldn't have been so strong. He always believed in the bond that they shared. Nobody except them could understand the faith they both had in their feelings. And for a while, just a little while, their faith had shaken.

Both of them had carved out their lives around that history. None of them tried to erase it from their lives. History was the reason they had their present.

Sameer asked Anaya to freshen up before meeting Riya while he completed some urgent work as they reached home.

He texted Riya that Anaya got permission to be home for the weekend and wants to meet her.

Anaya went to her room and took a bath. She went to Sameer's room to keep Riya's note in the blue box. As she opened the box, her eyes settled on one of the letters. She took that letter out and remembered it is from the letter girl. It had been really long that she had thought about her.

She remembered her dad telling her their story, and for such a long time, it had been in her mind. Just when she was about to keep the letter back, her eyes wandered to Riya's note in her other hand, and her eyes widened.

She looked at both the handwriting and exclaimed. They were the same handwriting.

She was ecstatic! It was like a discovery for Anaya. She felt as if she just solved a mystery that had been enveloping her ever since her dad told her about the letters.

She rushed downstairs to Sameer, who was hitting the keys on his keyboard.

"Ms. Riya is the letter girl?"

Sameer, taken aback by her sudden impatience, could not understand the context and what Anaya was trying to say. He turned around to face Anaya.

"The letters! They were from Ms. Riya?" Anaya was bouncing with excitement.

"What?" Sameer was still not able to grasp her excitement.

"Papa! Ms. Riya is the girl whose letters you have. She is the one you were in love with?"

And then it struck Sameer what Anaya was trying to say.

"I matched the handwriting of the note Ms. Riya wrote to me. They are the same. The letter girl is Ms. Riya! Isn't it?"

Sameer was not prepared for such a confrontation so soon. He had wanted to create a comfortable atmosphere and then explain it to Anaya. He had no idea how it would affect Anaya. He had been thinking of ways to tell Anaya about Riya. But he was not ready for such a disclosure.

Sameer nodded slowly and as cautiously as ever.

"No wonder you were so relaxed and cheerful whenever she was around. Is that how you knew so much about her?"

Sameer, unsure of the delicacy of the situation, just nodded along. He felt as if he had been caught in an illegal act.

Anaya's enthusiasm was defined by the fact that she could crack a mystery that had surrounded her.

"I cannot believe it! Ms. Riya. Does she know you have been looking for her?"

"Yes. She found out." Sameer realized it was the time that he told her everything.

"And? Does she still love you?" Anaya was bubbling with energy.

"Why don't you ask when we meet her today?"

"Will she tell me?"

"I think she will."

Chapter 54

"Ms. Riya." Anaya got down from the car and rushed to hug Riya. Riya wrapped her in her arms.

"Nice scarf." Riya smiled at Anaya.

"I love it. Thank you so much."

Anaya looked at Sameer with naughty eyes. Sameer instantly understood what she wanted to ask Riya. Looking at the two of them exchanging looks, Riya folded her hand and asked, "What are you two planning today?"

"Ms. Riya. I…I got your note too." Anaya hesitated.

Riya, unable to understand her hesitation, looked at Sameer for a clue. But Sameer just stood there grinning broadly.

"Thanks, darling. Did the principal scold your dad too much?"

"Not at all. He explains to her so well that she forgets to scold him. She loves papa."

Riya laughed at her innocence. "Everyone loves your papa."

"Really?" Anaya asked mischievously.

"Of course!" Riya was still unaware of what was happening, and before she could even understand, Anaya asked, "Do you?"

Astounded by her question, she looked at her, "What?"

"Do you also love papa?"

Riya looked at Sameer to take over, or at least help her out. She was panicking.

"Papa said you would tell me if you do," Anaya remarked thoughtfully.

Sameer was grinning. It was hard for him to control his emotions. He was intently watching the scene unfold between the two ladies who mean the world to him. Sameer gazed at Riya, and she knew the answer.

"Yes, honey. I do. I love your papa very much."

"Really?" Anaya was back to being excited. She clasped her hands and was looking alternatively at Sameer and Riya.

"Yes!" Sameer and Riya said in unison.

Sameer hugged the two of them tightly. He didn't realize he had tears in his eyes. He kissed Anaya and then kissed Riya and let out a sigh of relief. It felt as if he had been holding on to that breath ever since Riya disappeared from his life.

"Wow, papa. Will you marry her?" Riya coughed at such a direct question from a little child, but then she remembered how mature Anaya is for her age.

"I am not sure. Ms. Riya sleeps till late in the morning. And you know how particular I am about breakfast. Can you give me some princess advice?" Sameer tried to be his usual funny self, simultaneously teasing Riya.

"You should totally marry her. She is so awesome!" Anaya gleamed.

"Really?" Sameer tried to look skeptical.

"I love Ms. Riya. She is amazing."

Chapter 55

Days passed in a euphoric state. Sameer was unable to believe that he was going to marry Riya. He had dreamt of this day ever since they realized they were in love with each other. He knew his dream came at a price of twelve years but nevertheless, here they were, working on their vows.

They had wanted to keep it a small wedding on the beach. Anaya was home with special permission. She had to attend all her classes for an entire month before she was allowed.

Aarush had handled all the basic necessities. He had coordinated with his friend's restaurant at the boardwalk for music and appetizers.

Sameer was fidgeting nervously. He had no idea why he was so anxious. It was their day today, finally. He closed his eyes and tried to calm himself. The moment he opened his eyes, he saw Riya walking towards him, clad in her gown.

The determination in her eyes radiated towards Sameer. This was the girl who always believed in *forever.*

As she came closer, he bent forward and kissed her slowly.

"Vows." Anaya said.

They had dropped the conventional ways of marriage and agreed on asking Anaya to minister it.

"Papa." Anaya whispered.

Sameer nodded towards Anaya and then looked at Riya.

"I cannot start to tell you how blessed I feel to have shared my youth with you, Riya. I cannot bring back the lost years, but I promise to make it up to you with all my heart. I promise to grow old with you and experience life one breath at a time. Because my love, no one can make me breathe the way you do when you love me. I love you, today and forever."

Riya was smiling behind the tears.

"Riya." Anaya whispered.

"All my life, I have waited to be with you. I never knew love could come my way wrapped in the form of a best friend, again. The way you make me feel is something I fail to describe in words whenever I try. It is beyond the meanings that lay in words. I promise to be the reason for your smiles till my last breath. I love you."

"Now you may kiss the bride." Anaya whispered excitedly.

Sameer was gazing deep into Riya's eyes. He could see his entire world in them.

"Hey, dude! I can do that favor for you if you aren't so sure." Aarush mocked Sameer.

Sameer glared at Aarush as Riya laughed.

He stepped forward and kissed Riya and whispered, "I'll take care of you." Riya hugged him tightly and kissed him again.

Aarush got up from his seat and went on the makeshift dais.

"Hey, man!" Sameer was shocked to see Aarush coming up and asking him, the groom, to take a step back.

"You've done your kissing. Now it's my turn." Everybody gasped. Riya hit Aarush and glared at him.

"I mean, we have something for you, Sameer. Please have a seat." Aarush gestured him away and looked at the crowd, "May I please welcome our princess, Anaya."

"But…" Sameer was startled at what was happening.

Anaya pulled Sameer from his place and stood opposite Riya.

Aarush looked at both of them and asked if they were ready. "Okay! Repeat after me."

"I"

"I"

"Riya"

"Anaya"

"Take Anaya to be my lawfully adopted princess."

"Take Riya to be my lawfully adopted mommy."

Riya kissed Anaya on her forehead and hugged.

Sameer turned around, unable to believe what he just heard. He couldn't stop looking at the two girls who define his world. Riya and Anaya looked at Sameer and blew a kiss. Sameer wiped a tear off his cheek and rushed to embrace his entire universe.

More often than not, happiness is just a person! And so is life!

Epilogue

Riya!

Happy Birthday!

I cannot believe it has been years that I haven't been able to wish you on your special day. I remember how you loved to celebrate your birthdays. All those times, I promised myself that I will always be there to celebrate this special day with you. It seems I am not really good at keeping promises to you and myself.

In all my past letters, I have asked for your forgiveness. But now I have decided that I will only write to you about how much I love you. Because I know you believe in love more than any other feeling.

My little girl, Anaya, has grown up now. She is just like you. Sometimes I can see your glimpses in her.

Lately, I have been having a lot of dreams about you. Some are as heavenly as was your presence in my life, while some are sorrowful. But they always leave me with remnants of your memories. I don't know where you are or how your life has turned out to be. I wish I was still a part of your life. I know I am being selfish here because I don't want to imagine my life without you, but I wish I could still make you laugh.

You know, today morning when I opened my laptop, it displayed a beautiful beach. Do you know what was the first thought that I had? I imagined you walking towards me in a wedding gown. My eyes filled with tears looking at the aura that you radiated and the resolution in your eyes to be with me. You looked divine, Riya. And since then, I have been just thinking about the day we will get married. Call me foolish, but I know our love is strong enough to survive the years we are spending apart.

Someday I will make you my bride, Riya, because there is no other happiness more eternal than being with you for every moment of my life.

---The End is The Beginning of A New Phase---

Made in the USA
Columbia, SC
26 May 2021

38527222R00159